Plata o Plomo

JW ORCHARD

PLATA O PLOMO

For permissions, inquiries, or more information, contact: Info@JWOrchardBooks.com

Paperback ISBN: 978-1-970802-13-9

EPUB ISBN: 978-1-970802-12-2

Disclaimer

This book is a work of fiction created solely for entertainment purposes. All characters, organizations, events, and locations are products of the author's imagination or are used fictitiously. Any resemblance to actual persons, living or dead, or to real incidents, institutions, or organizations is entirely coincidental.

The scenarios, technologies, and actions depicted in this story are dramatized for narrative effect and should not be interpreted as accurate representations of real-world procedures, capabilities, or advice. The author and publisher disclaim any liability for any loss, injury, or consequences arising from the interpretation or use of the content in this work.

9 IRON MEDIA

DEDICATION

To my friend Tim and all of those in recovery, fighting the quiet battles with relentless courage. Those who choose the harder road. Stay in the fight.

ACKNOWLEDGMENTS

To my God, my wife, my family, and those who read these books. Many thanks to the people of Amarillo, Texas; Deadwood, South Dakota; Yellowstone, Wyoming; Moab, Utah; and Tombstone, Arizona, and to everyone I met along the way while researching this book.

I want to thank Ian Fleming, Lee Child, Ray Bradbury, and Stephen King, whose books I have studied and read.

I would like to thank my editor, Mike Valentine, as well as Debra and Kristina, for the time, effort, and thoughtful insight you invested in this story. Your contributions strengthened it in ways I could not have accomplished alone.

CHAPTER 1

San Antonio, Texas, was packed with people on a Saturday evening. Fiesta Con was just finishing up its one-day event at the downtown convention center, and the city's population had ballooned. Normally, the city's population was two and a half million, but now it topped three million. *Noches Calientes* had already begun. Most of them were downtown for the comic convention and the *Noches Calientes* street party that followed. The party started as an impromptu get-together of cosplayers and convention goers over the years. Someone finally decided to organize it. It wasn't just a party anymore. It had grown into a parade, and the rest was history.

People were everywhere, and the streets were clogged with traffic. The traffic had tempers simmering just below boiling, and the warm temperatures didn't help. Also, the crowds of people flowing randomly across the streets caused more than one driver to honk, yell, and some to give a one-finger salute.

Jerry Meegler was inside the San Antonio Convention Center packing up his booth. He was an up-and-coming YouTube personality who did a show on all things strange and unexplained. He and his fans discussed anything from cryptids to strange lights in the sky. Once he finished packing, he went to Greg Morris, who was a vendor in the booth next to him.

"Hey, man. I'm out," Jerry said.

Greg held a curtain open and waved Jerry to the back of the booth.

"I've got something for you before you leave," Greg said.

Jerry didn't answer and went to the back of the booth. Greg closed the curtain. He picked up a black plastic case and put it on a folding table. Greg flipped the latches and opened it.

Greg reached in and pulled out a small black egg-shaped case. He handed it to Jerry. On opening it, Jerry saw two small, clear earbuds. He put one in each ear and heard the AI voice announce that the earbuds were paired.

Jerry tapped his left ear and asked, "How do I sound?"

"Like you always do, unimpressed," Greg responded.

Jerry put on a black mechanic's shirt over his dark blue T-shirt, then a black-and-white baseball cap with the words "Los Spurs" embroidered on the brim. This would cover his spiked blonde hair.

He was in his early thirties, rougher around the edges than he had been a few years earlier, yet he still carried the bones of a good-looking man, a strong jaw line, straight nose, and pale blue eyes that saw more than he ever let on.

Jerry's hair was thick, light brown with blond undertones. Jerry usually kept a few days' worth of stubble, not as a style choice but because it suited him. He resembled a cross between a young Kiefer Sutherland and Kurt Russell.

He stood just under six feet with an athletic build, but not too big to give the idea he was a gym rat. His posture was relaxed in that specific way people get when they learned long ago not to show tension. There was a quiet vigilance to him, the kind developed from years of watching doors, watching people, and watching his own back.

Jerry wore faded jeans and scuffed boots. He moved with the easy confidence of someone who's been in more than a few fights and knows he doesn't need to prove anything.

He thought the cap plus his rough beard would help him blend into the crowds.

"Where is everyone else?" Jerry asked.

"In place." Then he motioned to the curtain and said, "Be careful."

"Always," Jerry said, gave him a weak salute.

Jerry turned and headed for a side exit. The main exits were crowded with people leaving for more fun and camaraderie. He pulled the brim lower as he went out of the exit to East Market Street.

He crossed East Market Street and walked up Bowie Street, heading to East Commerce Street, where a parade was going to be. The smell of cooked meat and bacon filled the air from Denny's on the corner of Commerce and Bowie.

The smell reminded him of his first meal when he got out of prison. Denny's was the first place he stopped. He ate a steak with fries and a chocolate milkshake. He thought it was the best meal of his life.

Once at the corner, a surge of noise to his right washed over Jerry, as *Noches Calientes* began under the I-37 bridge on Commerce Street, pulling him back to reality.

The street throbbed with drums, horns, and the hum of generators powering floats that looked stitched together with cloth and flowers. The air had the faint smell of marijuana, sweet grease, and burnt sugar. It clung to his skin, to his thoughts, to the edges of his resolve. He knew that smell all too well. Jerry had finally realized that nothing was more important than his sobriety.

Jerry's thoughts went back to the time he had spent in prison for a burglary he had committed to feed his drug habit. He thought of how hard he had fought to get the monkey of addiction off his back. He knew he would always be a recovering addict. Jerry shook his head, admitting that his life was better being clean.

A smile crossed his face as he thought about his trip to the Badlands to celebrate his friend Mark's one year of sobriety. He was going to give him his one-year sobriety coin. Jerry had sponsored Mark in his recovery. They had met at a comic convention a little over a year ago when Mark decided to get sober. A sponsor acts as part big brother and mentor. The sponsor explains what they went through and how they stay sober.

Mark wanted to celebrate by getting his coin in the Badlands National Park in South Dakota, under the stars of the Milky Way. Jerry thought it was a great idea. He hadn't been out there in years and would enjoy the ride. He put his hand in his pocket felt the one-year sobriety coin.

The convention crowd bled into the street festival, superheroes and Stormtroopers shoulder to shoulder with locals in sequined sombreros. Sweat gleamed on every face. Laughter and basslines tangled in the air. Somewhere above the noise, fireworks bloomed.

Jerry scanned the crowd. He wasn't there for the party. Control had intercepted chatter an ECLIPSE operative had embedded in the *Noches Calientes* parade, disguised as a mariachi guitarist—code named: *El Zorro Rojo.*

El Zorro was supposed to be carrying a biotech implant. It was called SPECTER, a Defense Advanced Research Projects Agency (DARPA) prototype built for special forces. Someone had stolen it before it was ready for deployment

It could rewrite thermal signatures, effectively making a person invisible to drones and infrared surveillance. Hidden beneath the skin, the device could broadcast faint interference.

The device could erase a person from every thermal scan and drone feed and effectively make them a ghost in plain sight. If it fell into the wrong hands, every cartel, mercenary, syndicate, and rogue network would want it. Smuggling, assassinations, warfare, could all be done with invisibility. The device was supposed to be turned over to another unknown operative and taken out of the country.

The briefing from Control had been light on details and heavy on warnings. "Use nonlethal force, before escalation, but under no circumstance must it fall into the wrong hands," he'd said.

Jerry's mouth was dry as he remembered. He could still taste the last coffee he'd drunk. The smell of smoke was not just marijuana. Something chemical, something wrong, teased at the edges of memory. His pulse stuttered, the old itch waking.

Jerry made his way down East Commerce Street to watch the parade. He stopped to read an alabaster plaque near a crosswalk close to the Statue of St. Anthony of Padua on the River Walk.

The engraving on the plaque read, "On this spot the bodies of heroes slain at The Alamo were burned on a funeral pyre. Fragments of the bodies were afterward buried here."

Jerry wondered what those men would think of him and the city that had eventually resulted from their sacrifice. He turned to watch the spectacle coming his way.

The parade made its way down the street, and the night was alive with music and lights. Trumpets blared from a mariachi band riding atop a flower-covered float, their notes tumbling through the warm air like sparks. A group of men and women led the parade dressed in Native American attire. They held paper lanterns suspended from poles that swayed overhead, painting everything in gold and crimson.

Behind them, a group of women danced ahead of the float. They all wore trajes de china poblana, the traditional Mexican dress. Their white blouses hugged their shoulders delicately. Each blouse had embroidered, multicolored, bright flowers.

The women's skirts were wide, made of deep red satin and rich green velvet, embroidered with brilliant designs of golden eagles, stars, and radiant bursts of color that flashed as the fabric flared with each turn. Around their waists, silk sashes were tied tight, their ends trailing with the motion of the dance.

The women represented every ethnicity, which is what made San Antonio so charming to Jerry. It has been said that San Antonio was the biggest small town in America.

They danced side by side, their skirts rippling in perfect rhythm, faces shining with sweat and joy. Their hair was braided and adorned with ribbons, marigolds, roses, and strands of silver thread woven between them. They spun and danced their way down the street.

Jerry noticed two Caucasian twin women in the group. He knew them like his own family and from many missions they had gone on together. They were known as the Acosta twins Samantha and Alexandra, but to him they were Sam and Alex.

Each had a unique talent. Sam was a producer of independent films and was also a polyglot, and Alex was a medical doctor. They fit right in with the beautiful women in the group. He thought they stood out, but maybe because he was biased.

Jerry also knew that if he saw them, then his target was close. They had discussed it in the mission briefing that they would be in front of their target. The question for him was how far in front?

The crowd cheered, clapping in time, as fireworks began to bloom overhead, red, green, and white. Jerry smiled as a small girl watched the women dance and spin, trying to imitate the dancing women as best she could.

A parade rolled past a float painted in crimson, gold, and fire colors. Another mariachi band followed on foot, the brass shimmering, guitar notes slicing through the humid night. Jerry's gaze locked on the man at the back, black charro suit, red sash, a silver guitar catching the light like a blade.

Over the man's shoulder, cosplayers walked, waving to the crowd. Name the genre, and you had someone dressed as a character. Stormtroopers and wizards walked side by side.

One of the cosplayers was dressed as Elvis Presley with sunglasses, a pompadour wig, and a sequined white jumpsuit with a cape. He looked like he had just jumped off the stage from Las Vegas.

Jerry knew his real name. This was Michael Sinclair, or as he preferred to be called, Mike. A former soldier, he had the gift of mimicking any voice he heard, but he loved impersonating Elvis.

Mike was waving to the crowd and looked right at Jerry. His fingers suddenly pointed up like twin pistols. He turned and pointed at the guitarist with the red sash.

Bang. Bang. He shot invisible rounds, each "shot" punctuated by a sharp thrust of the hips and a wink.

This was El Zorro Rojo. He was wearing a large black sombrero with silver embroidery, over his brushed-back dark hair and partially shading his tanned face. The man was broad-shouldered and wore a crisp, white tie, tied with a bright silk moño at the collar. Covering that was a traditional charro-fitted black jacket. Below that, an embroidered belt held up matching pants trimmed with silver and buttons. Finally, his black polished boots completed the look.

Jerry estimated he was about 5'10 "and a solid 180 pounds. That was the problem. El Zorro Rojo didn't look any different from any of the other mariachi performers that he had seen. On a night like tonight, there would be a lot of them. He had to keep close, or he might easily lose him in a crowd, Jerry thought.

Mike turned away and walked to the other side of the street and took a selfie with a woman in the crowd.

This was the last confirmation Jerry needed. He waited a moment as the mariachis passed by him. He stepped into the street. The crowd closed behind him like water. The twins and the Elvis impersonator were his PROACTIVE team. Greg Morris was also part of it. Greg was a former rapper and technical genius. He could build almost any gadget or device you needed. They had all been recruited by a man they only knew as Control.

Jerry remembered the day he was working at his first convention booth. A man in a wheelchair wearing a three-piece suit rolled up to his booth. The two discussed alternative timelines, cryptids, and so much more. Jerry thought it was odd that the man had so much knowledge. He offered Jerry a position as a communications specialist because of his YouTube channel.

Control had just asked him one question.

"Do you want to make a difference?"

Jerry didn't know how to answer. He didn't really believe that it was a real job. He was an ex-con and had no real skills.

He thought, "What do I have to lose," and accepted.

Three days later, he was in a mansion in the Adirondack Mountains, standing in front of Control's desk. That's when he felt he had gone down Alice's rabbit hole. One thing Jerry had noticed after all the years of working for PROACTIVE is that no one ever asked about his prison time or his addiction recovery. Also, he was given free time, even during a mission to go to a recovery meeting or contact his recovery sponsor if he needed. Jerry's team members respected his skills and didn't judge him about his past. The respect was mutual.

PROACTIVE was short for Preventing Rebellion and Organized Attacks Through International Vigilance and Counter-Espionage. They were between a quick reaction force and a balancing force against groups that wanted to cause harm.

Control liked to say they were akin to preemptive fighters. They fought to prevent a minor conflict from escalating into a much larger one, like firefighters starting a backfire. The firefighters intentionally set a smaller, controlled fire ahead of a wildfire's path. The goal is to burn fuel for the larger fire. That way, when the fire does arrive, there is nothing to burn.

There was only one catch. They weren't sanctioned by any government or law enforcement agency. Everything had to be done in the shadows, even if the bad guys didn't play by the rules. Jerry knew that sometimes you had to be very creative when working to thwart evil.

All of this went through Jerry's mind as he went with the motion of the crowd, keeping his eyes on *El Zorro Rojo.*

Jerry knew that Rojo would be meeting his contact on the River Walk, where the San Antonio River and the East River Walk meet. Lots of ways in and out there, and lots of different people. He thought back to his training in Open-Source Intelligence.

OSINT in motion, he thought.

If this were a desk job, he'd be pulling open-source feeds, tourist selfies, live-stream tags, geotagged vendor ads, and local traffic cameras. Out here, he had to improvise the analog version: the real-time human feed. Every detail was an open source. Every stranger was a data point.

The crowd grew thicker as it proceeded down the street. Jerry's view was obstructed for a moment as the parade turned left on South Alamo Street. He didn't see that Rojo turned left and headed north on Alamo Plaza. Once the crowd cleared, Jerry tried to find him. There was a new guitarist, but it wasn't Rojo.

Jerry darted to the corner of the Old Joske's building at the corner of East Commerce Street and Alamo Plaza, put his finger to his ear, and leaned toward the building.

"I've lost Rojo at Alamo and Commerce," he said slowly but clearly.

"Heads on a swivel," he heard Mike say.

"Proceed as planned," Jerry said as he scanned the crowd.

Halfway down Alamo Plaza, he saw Rojo. Jerry had to move fast before he lost sight of the man again.

"I've got eyes on him." Jerry started down the street after Rojo.

His mind raced, trying to remember the layout of Alamo Plaza. What he was now walking on used to be a street that ran in front of The Alamo. The surrounding area had been renovated into a pedestrian plaza. Jerry remembered that Blum Street intersected the plaza from the right and led back into the River Center Mall. Further up, Crockett Street intersected the plaza on the left. The crowds were thick as Jerry worked his way down the street, making it difficult for him to keep his eyes on Rojo.

He watched as Rojo passed Blum Street. A group of stumbling bachelorettes bumped into Jerry, soaking his right leg with their margaritas.

"Watch out, jerk!" one overly enthusiastic member said.

He felt the moisture, looked down at his leg, and kept moving. If Jerry had cared to look, he would have seen the rest of the group standing, looking put out and giving him a one-finger salute.

Rojo turned the corner at Crockett, heading west. By the time Jerry made it to Crockett Street, he saw Rojo disappear down a set of steps that led to the River Walk.

Jerry picked up his pace. *Where is he going?*

Once Jerry made it down the steps, he looked up and down the river. Lantern light shimmered across the water, breaking into scattered gold as colored river barges full of tourists drifted by, the guides giving a lively description of the sights and sounds.

The San Antonio River Walk started as a flood-prone bend in the river that was almost paved over until architect Robert Hugman imagined a sunken promenade one story below street level, with bridges, paths, and shaded waterways. Construction turned the area into a hidden, winding world beneath the streets, where cool air stayed, and stone steps curved down to peaceful water. Over time, it grew, adding cafés, hotels, and music-filled patios.

This part of the riverwalk was one continuous chain of restaurants with patio dining on the river. There were only two ways his prey could go. Left or right.

The crowds clogged the sidewalk that ran up and down this side of the river. Jerry took a minute and scanned every patio he could see and every passing face—no sign of Rojo.

He heard mariachi bands playing to his left. The problem was that it just wasn't one group playing on a night like this. Almost every restaurant had a mariachi or two playing for diners, and all of them were dressed almost alike.

Jerry looked at his watch. He knew the meeting under the bridge would be soon. He turned left as he made the decision to head to the rendezvous location. He did his best to look like a tourist as he passed the patios full of laughing, smiling tourists, dining beneath the colored umbrellas that blocked the sun during the day, under the shade of cypress trees. The earthy smell of the river, mixed with the smell of fresh tortillas and sizzling fajitas, filled the air.

Jerry kept searching for Rojo. *Where is he?*

He began breathing a little more heavily. Jerry slowed down. Up ahead at the Café Ole, he heard a guitar and violin start a rendition of "Cielito Lindo." He had lunch there during the pre-mission reconnaissance. Jerry slowed as he got closer.

Rojo and another man were playing for a table of people on the patio. Jerry tried to find a place to stop, but the crowd pushed him on. All he could do was go with the wave of humanity as he was pushed past Rojo.

The crowd thinned a bit as it reached the Commerce Street bridge. The bridge formed a huge man-made cavern over the river. It wasn't as well-lit as the rest of the river and gave Jerry a chance to move to the wall and let the crowd move past. He was trying not to be seen.

When he was in the yard in prison, he would find a place at the wall of the prison yard and try to make himself as unobtrusive as possible. He wasn't a coward. It was a matter of survival. Anything could get you beaten or stabbed. Sometimes, all it took was someone not liking the way you looked.

Jerry didn't try to communicate with his team. The target was too close, and he didn't want to bring any attention to himself. The music stopped, and he heard some light applause. He glanced toward Café Ole, just in time to see Rojo and the violinist step down to the riverwalk. The guitar was slung over his shoulder. His right arm hung over the sound box as if he were protecting something inside. Rojo and his companion were heading Jerry's way.

Jerry bent down to tie his shoe as Rojo and his associate passed by. He waited a moment to put his finger to his ear as he turned toward the wall.

"Rojo is moving toward your location. He has a friend who plays the violin."

Further ahead, where the rivers met, there was an open area in front of an elevator that took people up to street level, and an out-of-order sign was on the elevator door. A portable karaoke machine was playing "Love Me Tender" as Mike did his Elvis impersonation. The twins swayed in rhythm as Mike sang. Rojo and his partner approached the group. Mike looked at Rojo and stopped singing. The song kept playing the melody.

"Hey, amigo. Can I play your guitar?" he asked.

Rojo shook his head no. "Sorry, my friend, it's a family treasure."

Alex walked up to Rojo. "Really, how much is it worth?"

Rojo smiled. "You might say it's priceless."

Sam came up from behind him, blocking the violinist. The violinist tried to move past Sam, but now Jerry blocked his path.

"This will make such a cool meme." Jerry held out his phone and turned on its light. He made a point of shining the light in the violinist's eyes, then directly at Rojo.

"Please stop." Rojo put his hand up to block the light in his eyes.

In one smooth move, Mike moved up and took the guitar from Rojo. Not giving Rojo time to react, he ran up the stairs to the street out of sight.

Jerry gave chase, with the twins following him. Sam slipped and tumbled back down the stairs. Rojo and his friend stumbled over her, slowing them down.

Once Mike was around the corner, he thrust his hand between the strings into the guitar's soundbox. He found the device and pulled it out, breaking one of the strings in the process. He then tucked it into his waistband.

Jerry ran up to him and yelled. "Hey, give the guitar back."

Mike feigned fear, let the guitar drop out of his hand, and ran off. Alex made it to the top of the stairs with the others following. Jerry picked up the guitar and handed it to Rojo.

"Wow, who would have thought Elvis would steal a guitar?" Alex said.

"Stupid pendejo," Rojo's friend said.

Rojo looked at the guitar and the broken string with suspicion.

"Thank you," Rojo said as both men turned away and went back down the stairs.

Jerry and the twins walked south on Alamo Street. A dark blue minivan with tinted windows pulled up, and the side door slid open. Jerry and the twins climbed in, and the door closed behind them. Greg hit the gas, and they sped off south on Alamo Street. Mike, now wearing a black T-shirt and jeans, minus his wig, turned around from the front passenger seat.

He had a big grin on his face. "That went smoothly."

"When you fell, Sam, that really helped," Jerry said.

"I'm working on getting that Oscar," Sam laughed.

"Another great performance from the King," Jerry laughed.

Mike curled his lip and said in his best Elvis impersonation, "Thank you, thank you very much."

CHAPTER 2

The following morning, Jerry was at the Caliente Harley-Davidson dealership in San Antonio. Jerry stepped into the dealership still carrying the heat of the Texas highway with him. A black skull cap clung to his head, its fabric sun-faded from years of riding, and beneath it his blond hair was damp at the edges from the July heat. His T-shirt was a worn charcoal gray. The words "Live Free or Die" on the chest were cracked and faded from years of wear and washing. Over it, he wore a broken-in black leather vest, its edges softened by rallies, long-distance runs, and other rides. Jerry had stitched the patches from some of those rides with uneven precision.

His jacket, too heavy for a San Antonio summer, was folded over the strap of the saddlebag-style pack slung across his shoulder. Jerry's riding jeans were thick, dark denim reinforced at the knees, faded in streaks from sun and miles, and carried the faint grit of the road in their seams. He wore black, solid, scarred rider's boots, the left toe polished lighter where it had worked a shifter thousands of times. Finally, his gloves hung from his bag, shaped perfectly to his hands and dusted with the pale residue of the highway.

Jerry moved slowly through the showroom, the fluorescent lights glinting off rows of polished chrome. His reflective blue sunglasses were flipped around on the back of his head. If he had his way, he'd buy them all. Jerry paused, eyeing a Fat Boy motorcycle.

Maybe he'd open a dealership once he retired, he thought. Jerry figured that day wasn't far off. He couldn't picture himself working as a PROACTIVE agent into his fifties. A couple of thoughts flickered through Jerry's mind. He'd never asked Control about a retirement plan, and aside from Control himself, he'd never actually met an older PROACTIVE agent.

Jerry was brought back to the present by a voice off to his right.

"She sure is a beauty. I'm Gary. How can I help you today?"

Jerry turned to his right as a man in his late twenties approached, the gray

Harley-Davidson mechanic's shirt marking him as staff.

Jerry grinned. "Yes, she is."

"Looking for a new one?" Gary asked.

Jerry shook his head. "No, I already own a 2000 Night Train. I'm down here on business."

"Now that's a sweet bike, with the Twin Cam and the fat rear tire and the skinny, 21-inch front wheel," Gary said.

Jerry nodded his head. "Classy look and clean styling."

"You know we can ship anywhere," Gary said, still working to persuade Jerry.

Jerry put his hand up. "I know, brother, but I came here because you also have rentals."

Gary smiled and gestured over to a counter in the back of the room.

"Follow me. I'll get you hooked up."

Gary walked to the counter with Jerry close behind.

A young woman was waiting behind the counter. Her hair was a bright, bottled red, falling to her shoulders in loose waves. Her eyes were clear, sharp, green, quick, and observant. Her nose was small and slightly upturned, which fit her full lips. Freckles dusted the bridge of her nose and cheeks, giving her a warm look. She wore a fitted dealership T-shirt and worn-in jeans.

You could tell by the way she stood, she knew she had a toned body. A full-sleeve tattoo covered her left arm, with roses, gears, and what looked like some Egyptian hieroglyphs of the gods Anubis and Osiris. All of it was woven together. The colors were vibrant, and the artwork precise. Jerry knew work like that didn't come cheap. Not like some of the prison tattoos he had gotten.

Gary looked at the woman, "Kat, this is…"

Jerry stepped forward. "Jerry."

Gary had an awkward look on his face.

Kat looked at him and smiled as if she enjoyed his discomfort.

Jerry turned to Gary. "Don't worry about it man."

"Uh, yeah. Anyways, Kat, Jerry wants to rent a bike," Gary said.

"Sure, what do you want?" Kat asked with a mischievous smile.

Jerry picked up on the cue. "If I have my choice of rides."

Kat leaned forward, "Yesss."

Gary looked back into the showroom, as if he had seen a new customer.

Without looking back, he said, "Sorry, got to go," and drifted off to the showroom.

"I'm looking for a Fat Boy, black, with saddlebags," Jerry said.

Kat eyed him with a smirk. "Hard or soft?"

Jerry continued the flirting. "Hard is always better, but for this ride, soft leather."

Kat feigned a pout. "I was hoping I could show you some."

"Maybe when I come back," Jerry said with a smile.

"How long do you plan to be gone?" she asked.

"About two weeks."

Kat turned to the computer terminal and started to type.

After a moment, she turned the screen so Jerry could see it.

"If you get the deluxe package, full insurance, roadside assistance, the works, it will be $2,500.

Jerry pulled a credit card and his cover driver's license from inside his vest and handed them to Kat.

She held the license up to compare the picture to Jerry's face. On the license, it said his name was Jerry McCoy, from Pasadena, California. He had done this hundreds of times before on other missions. He wasn't too worried, but he always thought that one of these days he was going to run into someone who really did live on the street and the city he was pretending to be from. His planned response was that it was just a mailing address when he was homeless.

Satisfied, she looked at the credit card. Kat's brow furrowed. Printed on it was R.I.P.

She looked up at Jerry. "What does R.I.P. stand for?"

"Rest In Peace, Mobile Repair," Jerry grinned.

Kat burst out laughing. "Now that's funny."

She got a puzzled look on her face. "If you're a repair guy, where is your bike?"

"Oh, yeah. In the shop, getting fixed. Kind of like the plumber that has leaky pipes. There was a comic convention in town last night, and I wanted to go, so I had to fly here. I'm supposed to be meeting a buddy out west, and well, I need a bike for the ride," Jerry explained.

Kat nodded as her eyes looked off to the right as she went through the story in her head. It seemed believable enough to her. She turned her gaze back at Jerry.

"Give me about thirty minutes to have the bike prepped, and you can pick it up on the side under the orange awning." She pointed toward the front doors.

"Great," Jerry said.

She pointed to a large, dark brown leather couch in what must have been a waiting area.

"Have a seat while I get everything ready."

Jerry walked over to the couch and sat down. The sofa was comfortable. Jerry knew that he had a long ride ahead of him. He decided to get a few minutes of sleep in before the road trip. He closed his eyes, focused on his breathing, and felt the sleep overtake him.

CHAPTER 3

Jerry heard the buzz of the fluorescent lights, smelled bleach and puke, and heard voices in the common area. Other voices whispered from somewhere. He was in his prison cell waiting. This was release day, and he would be free in a few hours, his time finally served. That is, if something didn't go wrong, like someone wanting to fight him because he was getting released. His heart started to pump faster with anticipation.

Jerry felt a light tapping on the bottom of his foot. He didn't jump to his feet. Before opening his eyes, he let his senses work. He heard people talking. Jerry smelled the leather couch and a light perfume. Convinced he hadn't woken up in a prison cell, he let his eyelids open slightly.

He recognized the blurry outline of Kat. Jerry blinked the sleep out of his eyes.

Jerry smiled. "My, aren't you a sight."

"Hey, sleepy. Your bike's ready," Kat smiled.

Jerry stood up and stretched his back and arms.

She held out an envelope. "Did someone keep you up late last night?"

Jerry took the envelope. "Someone's more like it."

Kat turned away as she blushed. She didn't know how to answer.

"Well, um, follow me to your bike." Kat turned on her heel and headed to the front door.

Jerry reached down and picked up his satchel. He placed the envelope inside it to follow her out.

Something caught his eye. The flat screen mounted above the parts counter flickered with reflections of chrome and the subdued light. Most days, it played loops of custom builds and cross-country rallies, but today the channel was tuned to the local news. The low volume carried through the quiet showroom.

Jerry didn't intend to watch, but there was a shift in the anchor's voice, somber, weighted, that drew his eyes upward. He knew the change in tone was bad news. It drew his eyes to the screen.

The screen showed a narrow alley taped off at both ends. Two shapes had already been removed, but the scene still held the outline of tragedy. There was a smashed guitar on the pavement, and a close-up of a violin bow snapped clean in half, half-submerged in a water puddle.

The anchor spoke in that steady, practiced cadence that made the worst things sound strangely orderly.

"Police are investigating the deaths of two mariachi musicians found early this morning behind the Mercado del Sol district. The victims, a guitarist and a violinist, were discovered by vendors arriving to set up for the market.

Motive at this time is unknown."

Their photos flashed briefly across the screen, bright-eyed, smiling men frozen mid-performance, the kind of faces that didn't belong anywhere near an evidence bag.

Below them, a red ticker crawled relentlessly:

BREAKING: Two Mariachi Musicians Found Dead in Alley. Police Search for Witnesses. Motive Unknown.

Jerry felt a faint prickle of unease. Maybe it was the broken instruments. Perhaps it was the alley's darkness lingering even on a brightly lit screen. Or maybe it was that deaths like these that made him wonder. Was he responsible for their demise? No, he thought. Everyone makes choices. They chose poorly.

Jerry glanced once more at the TV, at the crushed sombrero being zipped into an evidence bag. He turned away and headed for the door.

Once outside, the sun was blinding as it reflected off the white concrete of the parking lot. Jerry reached up and put on his sunglasses.

The Fat Boy sat under the orange sail shade at the edge of the dealership lot. The sun pressed down on everything beyond the canopy. The shade cut the glare from the chrome. A few narrow streaks of sunlight slipped through the fabric above, crossing the tank and fenders as the breeze shifted the canopy. Each shift of the sun picked out a different line of the bike. The sun caught the wide front fork, the broad tank, and the solid wheels. The bike was painted black, with chrome accents on the front forks and exhaust pipes.

Kat stood next to it like she was a model for the yearly calendar. Jerry walked around the bike to check for any scratches or other defects.

She sure is a beauty, Jerry thought.

"Everything is in the paperwork. Don't worry, you'll be covered," Kat said.

He looked at Kat. "The kind of coverage that if I total it, I'm covered?"

"Yeah, but I would like it to come back in one piece," Kat responded.

Jerry grinned. "Because if it comes back, then I come back."

Kat couldn't hide her feelings this time. "Something like that."

Jerry put his satchel into the left saddlebag. He winked at her as he swung a leg over the Fat Boy and settled onto the leather seat. It was warm from the sun. His boots found the pegs by habit. Jerry thumbed the shifter with a quick tap, checking for neutral. The soft green glow on the dash told him it was.

He reached the tank console and turned the ignition to ON. The fuel pump hummed, a brief, low note under him. Jerry flipped the red switch on the right handlebar to RUN. The bike felt awake now, and waiting.

With his thumb, he hit the starter. The engine answered with a slow, grinding whir, then settled into a deep chug-chug as the cylinders caught and came to life. Then the familiar loping rumble that traveled up through the frame and into his hands. He let the engine settle, the idle evening out. Then he rolled his shoulders, tightened his grip on the bars, and got prepared to ride.

Kat moved out of the way as Jerry's boot lifted the kickstand before he rolled out. She watched as he began to leave the dealership.

The engine thumped steadily as Jerry eased out of the lot, each pulse carrying across the pavement. When he rolled on the throttle, the note climbed just enough to show the bike was moving, then dropped back into its deep rhythm as he headed for the street.

Jerry braced his left boot on the pavement as the bike angled just a bit as he waited for traffic to clear before disappearing down the highway.

The sounds around him were clearer without a helmet dulling them. The engine kept a low, steady pulse beneath him, vibrating through the seat and into his hands. The wind met his face in a broad, rushing wall of air, loud but natural, carrying little shifts in tone as he picked up speed or eased off.

Once he turned off Loop 410 to US 90 and headed west, he could smell the bike more sharply, warm metal, a faint touch of fuel, and the dry scent of the road heating under the sun. Passing fields brought hints of grass and dirt, and whenever a truck rumbled by, he caught a brief swirl of diesel and dust.

The Fat Boy thrummed under him, steady and familiar. The wind pulled at his hair and brushed his ears, and every bump in the pavement came up through the tires in small, predictable jolts. It was open and straightforward, the kind of ride where the world met him directly as the highway stretched ahead.

He rode through Castroville, up the hill, and after an hour of leaving San Antonio, he was finally in Hondo. He pulled into the local Chevron to fill up.

Hondo was a small Texas town west of San Antonio, shaped by its railroad roots and the steady rhythm of ranching life. Its streets were broad and straight, lined with older buildings that reflected the area's slow growth. The residents formed a humble, tight-knit community, where most faces were recognizable, and routines seldom changed. Hot summers, mild winters, and stretches of open land characterized the surroundings, giving the town a quiet, grounded feel beneath the vast South Texas sky. It had a unique feature of a regional airport.

Jerry finished his fill-up and drove through Hondo. He read the welcome sign that read, "This is God's Country. Please don't drive through it like Hell." He checked his speed and was careful to respect the speed limit. He also figured that there would be plenty of law enforcement to make sure he did.

At the edge of town, across the street from the municipal airport, there was a Dollar General. Jerry slowed, put on his left blinker, and turned into the parking lot. A dark blue minivan with tinted windows was sitting in the parking lot. Jerry pulled in and parked next to it. Greg got out of the van, followed by

Mike, Sam, and Alex.

They were dressed the way most people in their thirties did in South Texas, casual and ready for the heat. Greg and Mike wore jeans with light-colored polos, and their boots were slightly dusted from the parking lot. The women had on denim shorts, loose tops that moved with the breeze, and sandals. Alex had her cap pulled low, sunglasses tucked into her shirt.

Greg walked up. "Hey, buddy."

Hey," Jerry responded.

They shook hands.

"I guess you heard the news?" Jerry asked.

Mike nodded. "Yup."

Jerry looked at the group. "What now?"

"We've got some leads we're going to run down," Sam said.

Alex waved the group over to the back of the van. "We've got a plane to catch."

The group walked over to the back of the van. Alex opened the rear hatch, revealing a plain brown box measuring two feet by two feet.

Greg looked at Jerry and pointed at the box. "This is for you, bro."

Jerry walked up to the box and gave it a skeptical look. The rest of the group stood in a semi-circle around him. He opened the box and pulled out a flat black motorcycle helmet.

Jerry turned around and looked at the group. "I'm not a helmet wearer, and no place I'm going requires a helmet."

Greg spoke up, "We know. It's an Outrush R Modular Bluetooth Helmet. It's the ultimate hands-free sound and communication experience. There are triple-vented cooling, a fully integrated sound system, and Bluetooth 5.0 capabilities. It has wind noise reduction with an integrated speaker and microphone system that supports up to 4 riders.

"You just couldn't resist getting me something with technology," Jerry laughed.

"We also don't want you to crack that pretty face of yours," Sam said.

Jerry smirked. "Why, thank you. I didn't know you cared."

"Not really, but it sounded good," Sam laughed.

Mike stepped forward. "I ride, too. It may also help you protect your hearing."

"You can also pair it to your phone and listen to audiobooks or whatever on history and cryptids," Alex chimed in.

Jerry put his hand up in surrender. "Okay, I'll take it with me, but no guarantees I'll wear it."

Greg looked at his watch. "Party's over. He has a road trip, and we have a plane to catch. Half Blackjack Garrett should be here in about 10 minutes."

The group exchanged goodbye hugs. Jerry went over to his bike and put the helmet in the right-side saddle bag. He watched as the van left the parking lot and headed across the street to the municipal airport.

He had to admit that he really did care for them, and they really did care about him. He mounted his bike, started it, and headed back east on US 90 to connect to TX 173 north. His first major stop would be Amarillo, Texas, 500 miles away from Hondo.

The ride would take him across central and west Texas, and across the Permian Basin, and finally to Amarillo. Jerry knew there would be some great sights in the Hill Country, but once he hit the basin, there would be miles of flat ground from horizon to horizon.

He didn't mind the long ride. He was free, and that was all that mattered. He also knew he would have to stop along the way to rest. Even in Texas, driving a motorcycle at night was dangerous. Jerry wasn't so worried about other nighttime traffic. It was colliding with the occasional wild animal crossing the road, or a neighbor's cow that had slipped through a fence.

He knew a few places where he could stop and get some rest. One thing he didn't have was a bedroll. Jerry planned to pick one up on the way. Right now, he wanted as much distance from San Antonio as possible.

CHAPTER 4

Jerry arrived in Hondo at the southwestern edge of the Texas Hill Country at the same time a Learjet 28 was shutting down its engines on the parking apron of South Texas Regional Airport. The latches released with a muted clunk, the Learjet's cabin door swung outward and eased itself downward, unfolding into a narrow set of metal steps. A breath of cool, pressurized air slipped past the seal as it broke, carrying the faint scent of leather from inside the jet.

The pilot climbed down from the Learjet 28, the metal steps ringing under his worn boots. He was built like a fire plug—five feet, ten inches tall, with jet black close-cropped hair, and a mustache and goatee.

Sunlight caught his faded jeans and the edge of his navy polo shirt, still warm from the cockpit. The man put on his aviator sunglasses and let his eyes adjust to the blazing white reflection of the sun.

He paused on the tarmac, letting the roar of cooling turbines fade behind him, and took in the quiet stretch of the runway and the empty horizon.

The tarmac smelled like a mix of sunbaked asphalt and jet fuel, thick, warm, and a little metallic. The Texas heat lifted the scent of rubber from tires and the faint tang of hydraulic fluid, blending with dust and the dry, mineral smell of concrete cooking under the sun.

His name was John Garrett, or as his friends called him, "Half Blackjack" Garrett. John had earned his name through a mix of nerve, brilliance, and a bit of insanity forged in the Army. A quiet but relentless sapper, Garrett was the man who could find or rig an explosive with a surgeon's calm. His unit first called him Blackjack for his impossible luck and unreadable poker face, but that changed on his third deployment in Kunar Province.

Pinned in a valley with enemy fire pouring down from a fortified ridge, his squad's escape required more demolition gear than they had. Garrett improvised, laying half a loadout of charges with precise, calculated madness.

He synced everything to a single trigger and blew the ridge clean without burying his team alive, something no one else would've even attempted.

When a stunned captain asked how he pulled it off with so little, Garrett just shrugged. "Half the gear. All the win."

From then on, he was Half Blackjack, the man who could play with half a deck and still take the whole pot. Some said that he was playing with half a deck above the neck. Garrett had his own point of view. If it works, it's not crazy.

He looked around. The heat was already rising off the pavement even before noon. The terminal building appeared as a low, beige structure near the edge of the ramp, simple, rectangular, and easy to pick out among the hangars and service sheds. A couple of ground vehicles were parked nearby, unmoving in the bright sun.

The airport was formerly known as Hondo Army Airfield. It resembled a functional airport designed for general aviation traffic, quiet except for the occasional fuel truck or single-engine plane moving across the apron. The sky was clear, visibility was good, and the heat caused the distant edges of the runway to shimmer slightly. Above the door facing the apron, written in brown block letters: "HONDO ELEV. 930

Two flag poles were on the other side of the building. One flew the Texas flag, and the other flew the American flag. The flags fluttered in the occasional warm breeze.

A second man, wearing a navy-blue pullover, jeans, and boots, made his way out of the aircraft. This was John Williams. He was a former Marine and worked for Garrett. He was in his late thirties, stocky, and wore blade sunglasses. He was the second-in-command, or SIC. Most people would call him the co-pilot.

All 20-series Learjets are certified for two-pilot operation only. Unlike some modern light jets, they are not approved for single-pilot operation and cannot be flown single-pilot without a special exemption (none are usually issued for the 28/29). Charter operators, corporate operators, and insurance requirements all mandate a Pilot in Command (PIC) and a Second in Command (SIC).

Garrett was flying empty back from San Antonio. A private jet often carries passengers one way, but the aircraft still needs to reposition, either to return to its home base or go somewhere else for its next trip. If there are no paying passengers on that repositioning flight, it's called an empty leg.

Garrett and John stepped into the terminal, letting the door swing closed behind them. Out on the ramp, he could still hear the faint growl of the fuel truck easing into position beside the Learjet.

They approached the front counter where the airport manager was sorting paperwork. The manager was in his mid-50s, with sun-lined skin from years walking the ramp. His hair was gray at the temples, cut short, and he wore a collared shirt with the airport logo stitched over the pocket. His jeans were clean but well-worn, and a radio was clipped onto his belt. He moved with the steady pace of someone who knew every inch of the field and didn't waste steps. The airport manager looked up from the counter.

"Morning. You the Learjet out of San Antonio?"

His voice had the flat, direct tone of a man used to giving instructions over engine noise.

Garrett put his sunglasses on the top of his head. "Yes, sir. John Garrett and John Williams of We Care Aviation."

John, taking Garrett's cue. He put his sunglasses on top of his head.

The manager nodded toward the passenger lounge. Through the open doorway, Garrett saw Alex, Sam, Greg, and Mike waiting with their bags lined up in a neat row.

"Your group's already here. Been waiting about fifteen minutes," the manager said.

"Good. They are fueling now?"

The manager nodded. "Just started. The truck rolled up right after you came inside. Shouldn't take long."

"Perfect. We'll be ready as soon as they're done." Garrett responded.

The manager flipped a file closed. "Let me know if the passengers need anything: ice, water, or stowing bags."

"Will do. Thanks."

Garrett gave a brief nod as he and John headed toward the lounge, switching into departure mode as the passengers rose to meet them.

Garrett waved to the group. "I'm John Garrett, your pilot."

He pointed with his thumb to John. "This is the man taking the van back to San Antonio."

Greg stepped forward and handed John the van keys.

"I hope no one forgot anything," John said with a grin.

"Nope. We've checked and rechecked," Sam said.

"Okay then. I'll be heading out." John turned and headed for the manager at the counter.

Garrett watched him leave and then addressed the group. "We should be wheels up in thirty minutes. I have some administrative things to work out. Mr. Morris, if you will follow me."

Garrett and Greg went back to the counter to wrap up the basics with John Williams, and the airport manager. They confirmed the updated crew lineup with Greg replacing the outgoing second pilot, verified the now three passengers and their bags, and signed off on the fuel slip for the top-off that had just finished on the ramp. With the manifest noted and the ramp fee waived thanks to the fuel purchase, the manager handed back the paperwork with a nod, leaving them clear to load up and get the Learjet moving.

The group boarded the plane and flew north toward New York State. They would take the device back to PROACTIVE headquarters in the Adirondack Mountains. The flight would take about five hours.

Once they reached cruising altitude, Greg turned to Garrett and hit the intercom button on his headset.

"What's the plan with the SPECTER?"

"Williams will take it to our lab, scan it, wipe it clean of prints, and return it to DARPA," Garrett said.

"I can't wait to see once inside. I can also develop a countermeasure," Greg said.

Below them, somewhere in west Texas, Jerry was getting back on the road after stopping at an old army surplus store to get a wool blanket and an olive-green poncho for his bedroll.

Farther west, a cell phone was vibrating in the pocket of a leather biker vest.

CHAPTER 5

The Buckskin Raiders' clubhouse bar, called The Raider's Den, was located south of Tucson, Arizona, near Elephant Head. It was about halfway between Tucson and Nogales, Mexico.

Inside, outlaw country blared so loud it vibrated the floor, the air thick with beer, smoke, leather, and gun oil. Neon lights smeared across chrome parts bolted to the walls. Most of the gang was present, each wearing his cut with pride. The place buzzed with sharp laughter and low arguments. The sound of pool cues cracking rose above the din. The glare of the light over the pool table obscured the players' faces. Only the players' muscled, tattooed arms could be seen.

Some men leaned against the walls, drinking and talking. Women in tight tank tops and cut-off shorts moved through the crowd, tattoos flashing on arms, ribs, and thighs.

A few sat on the laps of men sitting on stools at the bar. A busty female bartender wiped down glasses that never looked clean, her eyes tracked newcomers the way a guard dog sizes up strangers. In here, you don't just enter. You were judged the second the door shut behind you.

Frank Colt sat alone at the far end of the bar beneath the mounted horns of an old long-horn steer, sitting upright with his tailored black leather jacket open just enough to reveal the dual Colts cross-draws in his waistband. His last name was just a coincidence.

He was lean and wiry. When he stood, he measured an even six feet. At forty-five, he wore his hair slicked back. There were early streaks of silver beginning to show in his dark hair.

He also wore a cut, but his had the PRESIDENT patch on the upper right.

His sharp jaw and trim mustache framed ice blue eyes that looked older than he was, eyes that missed nothing and forgave even less. Though motionless, he exuded quiet danger of a man who trained daily and never let his reflexes dull.

The twin Colt revolvers tucked cross-draw into his waistband weren't decoration; everyone in the Buckskin Raiders knew he could out-think, outshoot, and outlast any man in the bar. Young for a president, yes, but the omniscient truth was simple. No one questioned why he held the position. Frank Colt didn't rule through volume or force. He ruled because everyone in the room understood he could drop them before they finished drawing breath.

The large flat-screen TV above him flickered with a breaking-news banner. Federal agents raided a counterfeit warehouse in El Paso, where pallets of forged documents and counterfeit designer gear spilled across the parking lot.

Frank watched without blinking, his eyes reflecting the images as if he were studying an autopsy of someone else's mistake. Around him, his men pretended not to notice the news report.

He had done time for robbery in his twenties. Once in prison, it became a university of crime for him. He was given a job in the print shop where he learned how to counterfeit almost anything, and more importantly, how to distribute it.

Frank Colt didn't leave prison reborn. He left refined, sharpened, with a purpose. Eight years inside had stripped him of recklessness and replaced it with a patient, coiled intelligence that made men twice his size step aside.

For strategic reasons he earned a degree in Business while serving his time. If he was going to build an empire of counterfeit IDs, passports, birth certificates, luxury knockoffs, and even antique-style Confederate notes, he needed structure, logistics, and a shield strong enough to keep Federal eyes looking in the wrong direction.

A motorcycle club would do nicely, loud enough to distract, common enough to disappear into, and obedient enough, if chosen well, to keep his actual business untouched.

The seed for the club came from the prison library. Frank found a biography of Buckskin Frank Leslie, an Old West gunfighter with more bodies on his ledger than most outlaws survived to count. One thing that stood out to Colt was that Leslie was reported to be only 5'7". The man's reputation was far taller than his actual size.

Some disagree on how many he killed. However, one notable person that Leslie killed was Billy Claiborne, the same Billy Claiborne who ran away at the O.K. Corral shoot-out. Claiborne told anyone who would listen that Leslie had killed Johnny Ringo. There is no verified evidence that Leslie killed Ringo.

Ironically, Claiborne died in Tombstone only a year and 19 days after the famous shootout, when Leslie shot him. That has been verified. Colt thought maybe Claiborne should have kept his mouth shut.

Colt didn't admire the killings. He admired the certainty. Leslie was a self-made man with a very colorful past. By the time Frank finished the book, he wasn't just inspired. He had a blueprint. Power wasn't about size. It wasn't about noise. It was about moving through the world with the unshakeable belief that no one could stop you.

His closest allies were forged behind bars. Royce "Vice" Moran, his calm, calculating cellmate, became the only man Frank ever trusted with strategy. Robert Mango, massive, scarred, and loyal for reasons Frank never quite understood, served as his protection.

Maybe because Mango had never had anyone he could call a friend, he became his Sergeant-at-Arms. Between them, a hierarchy had already formed long before any of them saw the outside world again.

Upon release, Frank named his new brotherhood the Buckskin Raiders, tipping his hat to the gunfighter who had taught him how myth becomes power. The name wasn't a claim of bloodline, just intention. Men remembered legends, and Frank Colt intended to become one.

There was more to Frank and the Buckskin Raiders. In Frank's mind, the Buckskin Raiders were not a motorcycle club. They were a counterfeit syndicate structured like a corporation, enforced through discipline and loyalty. The club was more like a corporation with handlebars. He built it on discipline, loyalty, and cold efficiency. Frank had learned both from textbooks and prison yards.

Royce and Mango were his closest allies.

Frank knew there were millions to be made in watches, purses, T-shirts, and nearly anything. But the one thing that made the most money was counterfeit documents. Birth certificates, passports, auto insurance, practically any official document. The two things he didn't mess with were drugs or counterfeit United States currency.

Frank knew the Federal maximum penalties for counterfeiting were generally 15 years. If drugs were involved or believed to be terrorism related, he could get 30 years. Finally, counterfeiting Federal currency carried a sentence of 20 to 25 years. Counterfeiting was the jurisdiction of the Secret Service.

One final factor was the cost of materials versus the return on investment. He could make 1000 times what he invested. There wasn't the headache of chemical transport or distribution networks. His stuff was sold at flea markets in the less obvious places of a city or town. Tattoo parlors made great fronts to meet potential document buyers. He stayed low and out of sight of the Federal law enforcement radar.

Others were more than happy to make themselves a larger target. It never worked out for them. Frank knew if you kicked the hornets' nest, they would keep hunting you down until they finally caught you. Ask anyone in the Supermax.

His phone vibrated in the breast pocket of his vest, sharp, insistent, like a living thing demanding attention. Frank didn't move at first. He let it buzz again, and a third time, before sliding two long, steady fingers into the pocket. He drew the phone out slowly, deliberately, as if the call were a gunfight he'd been expecting all day.

He didn't answer immediately. He glanced once at the TV as the agents hauled crates stamped with a counterfeit Texas birth certificate watermark suspiciously similar to a design his crew used just last month. He looked at the number, and his jaw flexed.

Frank thumbed the screen and lifted the phone to his ear. "Talk."

The members and patrons somehow knew to quiet down, and the music suddenly stopped. Whatever came through that line, every man present knew it could decide whether tonight ended with a meeting… or a war.

"When?" Frank said.

He listened. "Where?"

Frank hung up the phone. He turned to the others in the bar.

"Sergeant at Arms. Clear the bar. Only members present for this meeting."

A man known only as Mango, a massive man with arms the size of his legs came forward and roared, "You heard the man. If you ain't a member, get out. No old ladies, no nomads, nobody but family."

Outlaw motorcycle clubs follow a strict hierarchy based on loyalty, longevity, and proven commitment. At the top is the President, a position earned only after years of respected service and the trust of the entire chapter; he leads the club and makes final decisions. The Vice President rises beside him by demonstrating steady judgment and reliability, ready to handle disputes or step in when leadership is needed. The Sergeant-at-Arms earns his place through toughness, discipline, and the ability to enforce the club's rules without hesitation. The Road Captain attains his role by mastering the open road and proving he can safely guide the pack during rides. Administrative roles such as Secretary and Treasurer are given to members who have demonstrated responsibility, organization, and honesty over time.

Beneath the officers are the fully patched members, who have earned their patches through unwavering loyalty and years of brotherhood. Below them are prospects who must prove their worth through hard work, obedience, and dedication before being considered for full membership. At the bottom are hangarounds, newcomers who linger at the edges of club life in hopes of being noticed and invited to prospect. Each position is not just given, it is earned. The gang is a brotherhood that demands loyalty and respect.

The women, including the bartender, stopped what they were doing and left through the front door. The place was cleared in less than five minutes. Two members guarded the front door: one outside so no one could hear, and one inside in case someone tried to run. The back door was guarded the same way.

Once Mango had checked everything, he came back into the main room.

"Place is clear, and the guards are posted."

Colt nodded with approval. He turned to the remaining group.

"Ringo wants a conventus. He thinks he's so smart with his Latin. For the rest of you, a conventus is a friendly meeting."

The sound of knuckles cracking and guns being checked could be heard as the feeling of tension and anger swept over the bar.

"There's never anything friendly about a meeting with the Cowboys. Hell, they think they are God's gift to the world," one of the members said.

A murmur of agreement went through the crowd. Colt held his hand up in agreement.

"I said he wants a friendly meeting. It doesn't mean we have to give it to him," somebody said.

The others nodded and murmured to each other, grinning.

Colt held up his hand to silence them. "But violence is not good for business. Look what happened in Vegas a few years ago when two gangs got into it on the Strip. We don't need that kind of heat."

The group nodded in agreement.

"I'm going to need a lot of you on this one. He wants to meet in Deadwood, South Dakota. The rest of you, I need to stay and keep the money coming in. We leave tomorrow. I'll have names by tonight. Sergeant-at-Arms, open the bar back up. I want Tommy as my road captain, and Royce my vice-president in the back room."

Everyone nodded to acknowledge the orders.

The back room was soundproofed and for good reason. This was where the real gang business took place. Royce and Mango sat around a heavy, dark oak table. The Buckskin Raider logo was carved into the top. The person who did it was a master craftsman.

Royce Moran was a tall, lean man with the kind of build that came from years of hard living, not gym memberships. His black hair was kept short, a habit he kept from prison, and a matching trimmed beard gave him a sharper, older look. A thin scar ran from his left eyebrow toward his cheek, the only visible reminder of the fight that made him forever loyal to Colt.

Four guys jumped him in the yard, and Colt and Mango waded in to make it a fair fight. When it was over, Colt, Royce, and Mango were left standing. Their four opponents lay bleeding at their feet. The trio got sent to solitary confinement for a month, but when they came out, the prison world knew they meant business.

His gray eyes were steady and unreadable, always watching, always calculating. He dressed simply, in dark jeans, a plain shirt, and his Vice-President cut worn square on his shoulders. Royce wasn't the loudest or the biggest man in the room, but there was a calm, deliberate weight to him that made people pay attention. He looked exactly like what he was, the perfect right-hand man for Colt. He understood how Colt thought and executed commands without question.

Colt laid out a stack of crisp, freshly printed replica Confederate bills in different denominations. He picked up one and held it for Mango and Royce to see.

"All right," he began, "time for school. Don't worry, there's no test. You would fail anyway."

Mango and Royce looked at each other with a puzzled look.

Colt grinned. "You know that since the beginning, we have been looking for a way to go legit."

Mango and Royce nodded in agreement.

Colt held up a Confederate note and spoke.

"This isn't money the way you were taught to think about it. This bill matters only to those who already work with us. Inside our circle, the note can be traded for drugs, guns, fuel, or protection because everyone knows I will honor it.

Outside that circle, it's just paper."

Colt explained that no one was allowed to print, copy, or redeem it except through his people, which kept the supply tight and the value steady. If a biker crew wanted out, they brought the notes back through Colt's channels and exchanged them for real cash or product. No banks, no receipts, no records. As long as the money stayed inside the loop, it stayed useful, and as long as it stayed useful, Colt stayed in control.

"How will we know which ones belong to us?" Royce asked.

Colt slid a replica bill across the table. "What do you see?"

Mango leaned in. "A Confederate $5 bill."

Colt pulled out a UV pen light and shone it on the bill. "And now?"

Under the UV light, a single violet circle about the size of a quarter appeared on the right side of the bill. There was a circle split clean down the middle, with a coin on one side and a bullet on the other. He didn't raise his voice.

"Daylight, it's just paper," Colt said. "Under the right light, it tells you how this works. You take the silver, or you take the lead. There isn't a third option."

"This is how we move forward. No running. No hiding. We build something that doesn't get us in trouble. We use our heads instead of fists."

Mango scratched his chin.

"So… we're goin' from bikes and bars to… art dealers?"

Royce shrugged with a grin.

"Hey. If it pays the bills and keeps us outta handcuffs, why not?"

"When we finally make enough money, we disappear, we can pass the gang on to someone else."

The men chuckled, and the tension in the room eased. For the first time, the idea of a life outside the gang didn't sound impossible.

Colt stood, gathering the replicas.

"Listen. We're takin' history, and doing it on the up-and-up. That's the future. Not a crime. Not chaos. Just business—and this time, it's clean."

Royce whistled softly.

"We are becoming bankers."

Colt grinned.

"The other outlaws need to put their money somewhere. We like any bank keep a maintenance fee. What we are making is what used to be called a traveler's check.

"The money is paid for before it is ever circulated, and the watermark is proof of whether it is real and whether it belongs in his system. If someone tries to use it without access to the light or with people who don't recognize it, the bill is worthless.

"If it gets stolen or confiscated, we don't chase the paper. The holder reports it through our people, let's say through you, Royce, the serials are flagged, and those notes are dead the moment anyone checks them. The value doesn't disappear. It goes back to the owner.

"We reissue the amount in new bills with fresh serial numbers. The old ones are burned to remove them from circulation for good. Law enforcement could seize the paper, photograph it, and log it as evidence, but it's just paper. The value lives with us, not the bill, and the law could take the paper but never touch the real money."

Mango now understood. Just like contraband on the inside, the replicas had value only in the system.

"Get used to it. The world is changing. And so are we. I didn't spend all that time in prison to go back inside," Colt said.

"Just one question," Royce said.

"Go on," Colt replied.

"Do we tell the others?" Royce asked.

"No, this doesn't leave this room. When the time is right, I'll let them know," Colt said.

The two men nodded in agreement.

"Mango. Go tell Tommy I want to see him for the ride," Colt said.

Mango nodded, stood up, and left the room, leaving Royce and Colt alone in the room. Once the door was closed, Colt put everything away.

"What's the next part?" Royce asked.

Colt reached under the desk and handed Royce a letter-sized envelope that was filled with replicas of Confederate currency.

"Those are what they look like."

Royce opened one of the envelopes and let his thumb fan the bills.

"You can get these everywhere."

"These are the first set. That's the beauty. They are everywhere. We can move undetected. We control who gets them," Colt said and continued, "I need you to go to Tombstone, Arizona, and make sure the old Unified School conversion is on schedule. Remember, no colors, no bikes. You're just a guy who wants to help out kids learn a trade. Hire who you need to, but make sure it looks legitimate."

Royce looked at Colt with a smile.

"Got it. I turned my life around in prison, and my deceased aunt left me some money on the condition I use it to help others."

"One of Ringo's guys is going to bring the printing plates to Tombstone by the end of the week."

"Why are you depending on him?" Royce asked.

"These are the proofs I had made. There were a few things I wanted to add. The engraver said it would be a week. I've got to pay his frick'n toll tax, so I might as well hire one of his couriers to deliver."

Royce nodded in understanding. Colt reached over and picked up the replica $5 bill and handed it to Royce.

"Make sure you take this too," Colt said.

Royce took the bill and stuffed it into the envelope. He tapped the envelope against the side of his head. "See you in a week."

Back in Texas, the sun was getting low in the west as Jerry was pulling into the Big Texan RV Ranch. He'd heard about the place from his time in prison. Everyone called the guy Talking Texan. The guy talked constantly about

Amarillo. He told Jerry that if he ever got out, he should visit the place. Jerry wondered if Talking Texan ever got out of prison.

At least I finally made it to Amarillo, Jerry thought.

The RV park stretched out beneath the open Amarillo sky. Jerry thought that it looked like a small frontier village designed for wanderers. Rows of RVs rested under the setting sun beside neat gravel paths, while the ranch's rustic buildings gave the place a touch of Old West charm.

From its wide, easy pull-through sites to the welcoming office with its Texas-sized hospitality, the ranch felt less like a stopover and more like a friendly outpost along the highway's long trail.

The air carried a faint scent of mesquite and dust, and travelers coming and going added a quiet, ever-shifting rhythm to the grounds. Talking Texan said some of the best-known Route 66 attractions were in Amarillo. One of them was The Big Texan Steak Ranch, famous for its 72-oz steak challenge. If you can eat it with all its extras in an hour, then it was free.

Jerry went to the office. A young woman looked up as he entered, a warm, easy smile touching her face. She had that clean-cut North Texas look, blonde hair falling in loose waves to her shoulders, and clear blue eyes.

Her crisp white button-down Western shirt was worn in just the right places, tucked neatly into a pair of well-fitting blue jeans that showed she spent plenty of time on her feet. A simple leather belt and scuffed boots completed the picture. Nothing flashy about her, just a natural beauty. Jerry wasn't sure if it was her smile or just a feeling that made her immediately likable.

After hours on the motorcycle, Jerry looked like he'd ridden straight out of a sandstorm. His goggles left pale circles around his eyes, the only clean patches on his face. Everything else was filmed with road dust. The bandana over his mouth and nose was damp and dark with sweat, and when he pulled it down, the skin beneath showed deep pressure lines. His hair stuck out in wild, wind-blown clumps, and when he spoke, his voice carried that dry, rasping edge of a man who'd been breathing highway air all day.

"Been riding for a while?" she asked in a cheerful voice.

Jerry saw himself in a mirror behind the counter. He laughed at himself, realizing what he looked like.

"Yeah, I was wondering if you had a place I could camp for the night?" Jerry asked.

"We do, but you might want to stay in one of our converted Conestoga wagons?" she asked.

Jerry's face lit up in surprise. "Um, a what?"

"Think of it like a big wagon that's been converted for overnight stays. We decided to turn some wagons into a rustic hotel room. Each wagon has a door on the front. The wagon is outfitted with electricity, a refrigerator, a coffeemaker, a bathroom with a shower, and a bed," she explained.

Jerry unconsciously rubbed his back.

"You know that sounds good. I could use a good shower and a bed."

"Once you're cleaned up, we also have a shuttle that will take you to the Big Texan Steak Ranch," she added.

Jerry felt his mouth water at the sound of a steak and baked potato close by.

"Sounds like a deal I can't turn down."

The woman pointed to the door behind him.

"Just sign up. The shuttle leaves every half hour until 11 p.m."

Jerry turned to see where she was pointing. Then he turned back to the woman.

"How much do I owe you?"

"A little over a hundred," she said.

Jerry paid, collected his key, and left. He stopped to sign up for the shuttle, then looked at his watch. He figured he had just enough time to take a quick shower and change before the shuttle left.

Jerry drove his bike over to it and parked in front of the Conestoga. It resembled a Prairie Schooner, a lighter, more travel-friendly descendant of the Conestoga wagon. Almost every American Western has portrayed the schooner in wagon trains. While the Conestoga was a large, heavy freight wagon built for hauling tons of cargo over rough terrain, Prairie Schooners were smaller, more agile, and more common on long westward migrations such as the Oregon Trail.

Jerry opened one of the saddlebags and pulled out his overnight bag. He pulled out a clean pair of jeans, underwear, socks, and a clean gray pullover.

He walked up the stairs, used his key, opened the door, and stepped inside. The cool wave of air wrapped around him, sharp enough to raise goosebumps. The air-conditioning carried a faint metallic chill, the kind that cleared your head and dried the sweat on your skin in seconds.

He breathed in deeply, cool, clean, almost sweet air after the baked-dust smell outside. He felt the heat slide off him as the door swung shut behind him. Within minutes, he had stripped off his clothes and was in the shower. Under the shower, Jerry felt the road start to slip away from him. The hot water hit his shoulders first, loosening muscles that had been locked tight for hours. Dust and sweat ran off in thin, muddy streams, spiraling toward the drain.

He braced one hand on the shower wall and let the warmth soak into his back, easing the ache. For the first time all day, he breathed without the taste of wind and grit. Little by little, the tension leaked out of him, leaving a heavy, grateful calm in its place.

CHAPTER 6

The sun had set, and the night sky was full of stars above the abandoned stockyard. A light wind blew as the low rumble in the distance grew louder.

Headlights burst over the horizon as the first motorcycles roared toward the stockyard, illuminating the surrounding desert and yard through the gaps in the fencing.

Johnny Ringo's Cowboys stormed into the yard, engines snarling like a pack of wolves. They swung their bikes into a tight semicircle on the far side of the yard, exhaust fumes drifting through the headlights. One by one, their engines cut out, leaving a low growl of tension behind them.

Moments later, another wave of sound and light rose on the opposite horizon.

Colt's Buckskin Raiders entered in a sweeping arc, their customized Harleys shining with silver accents, leather tassels snapping in the wind. They formed their own semicircle facing the Cowboys, two crescents of steel, pistons, and barely contained violence.

The space between them felt ancient, like a dueling ground carved out by centuries of grudges.

From each semicircle, a single rider advanced.

Johnny Ringo rolled forward on his custom Harley-Davidson, matte-black, Fat Boy, dust billowing behind him. Colt matched his pace on a charcoal-silver Harley, the chrome caught the headlights like a drawn blade.

They braked within twenty feet of each other.

They dismounted at the same moment, boots striking the ground with deliberate, echoing finality.

Two modern kings stepping into the no-man's land between armies.

Johnny Ringo stood six feet tall, at his full height, with dark hair slicked back. His neatly trimmed mustache sharpened his defined jaw. Pale gray eyes locked onto Colt and didn't waver, holding that steady, assessing stare. Johnny wore a custom black leather jacket left open over a fitted dark T-shirt, matching leather pants, and tight black gloves that creaked faintly as he flexed his hands. A heavy belt rode low on his waist. An automatic pistol was tucked confidently at the waistband as if it were part of the outfit. As he walked forward, with his shoulders back and chin level, there was a faint, assured smile on his mouth, not friendly, not threatening, just sure he was about to be taken seriously.

The two couldn't be more different. The only thing they might have in common was their intellect. But neither man would concede that if asked.

For a long breath, neither spoke. The only sound was wind rattling the cattle chutes and the ticking of cooling engines.

Johnny broke the silence.

"You wanna explain," he growled, "how the hell our courier ends up dead in a gutter with no Specter on him?"

Colt's jaw flexed, but his tone stayed cool.

"I was hoping you could explain it."

Johnny stepped forward. "You sent him."

"You picked him," Colt countered. "Your man vouched for him."

Johnny's men bristled behind him, shifting like hounds itching for a command. Colt's Raiders mirrored the movement, hands drifting toward belt buckles, knives, and handguns.

Colt spread his hands, palms outward.

"The courier leaves with the Specter. Hours later, he's found with his buddy, shot. No device. No trail. No witnesses."

Johnny's voice darkened. "And you expect me to believe that's a coincidence?"

"I expect you to consider all possibilities," Colt shot back. "Could've been the buyer. It could've been another crew following us. It could've been someone overhearing us planning the handoff. Hell, could've been someone you pissed off last year. Your list of enemies is long."

A few Cowboys muttered curses at that, but Johnny lifted a hand to silence them. They fell silent.

He stepped closer, boots crunching gravel.

"Listen, Colt," Johnny said, quiet enough that the wind could've swallowed it. "The Specter isn't just some trinket. It's power. It's leverage. With that thing, we could rewrite the whole playing field. Someone knew what we had, and they took it."

Colt pivoted slightly, watching Johnny without blinking.

"Or someone in this very yard decided the payout was better solo."

Johnny's lip curled. "You accusing me?"

"If I were accusing you," Colt said, leaning in just enough to draw breath from both crews, "we wouldn't be having this conventus."

The tension between them tightened, pulled thin as wire.

The Cowboys' semicircle angled forward. The Raiders mirrored them.

Only the last thread of Johnny's discipline and Colt's restraint kept the two armies from crashing into each other.

Finally, Johnny took a slow step back.

"So here it is," he said. "The Specter's gone. The courier's dead. And whoever took it is out there, using our confusion to run circles around us."

Colt nodded once. "At least we agree on that."

Johnny pointed at him.

"But listen close. If I find out you knew more than you're saying, or if you played me, I'll drag your minting operation into the dirt and make you watch it burn."

Colt's smile was thin and dangerous. "And if I find out you tried to keep the Specter for yourself… I'll bury you with the courier."

A long silence.

Then both men turned, synchronized in their disdain, and mounted their motorcycles.

Engines roared to life. The two armies answered with their own thunder.

The Cowboys peeled away first, kicking up a wall of dust. The Raiders followed, silver glinting through the haze as they vanished into the night.

Colt smiled, thinking as he rode away. *Only a few more pieces in place, and Johnny's going to be history, just like his namesake.*

Johnny, riding in the opposite direction, laughed at the thought of watching Colt's entire operation go up in flames right before his very eyes.

By the time the confrontation had ended, Jerry had taken the shuttle to the Big Texan Steak Ranch and was waiting for his reservation. He had about twenty minutes to kill before he could be seated. He wandered through the gift shop. Nothing really struck his fancy. He just wasn't a souvenir kind of person.

From there, he made his way over to a shooting arcade. The arcade at the Big Texan Steak Ranch sat just off the main dining hall, illuminated with bright carnival lights that flashed against its Old West facade. Wooden cutouts of cowboys, coyotes, cattle, and outlaw silhouettes lined the back wall, each wired to jump, spin, or clang when hit.

The air carried a mix of sawdust, popcorn, and the faint electrical smell of the arcade rifles, .22-caliber style air guns bolted to the counter, their barrels cold and heavy but harmless enough for tourists. When someone pulled the trigger, a sharp metallic *ping* echoed through the room, followed by mechanical whirs as targets lit up or triggered tiny animatronic scenes.

There was a jittery saloon piano, a dancing cartoon cowboy, a rattlesnake that shook its tail and hissed. Kids laughed, adults missed shots they thought they'd make, and the whole place felt like a throwback to a state fair. It was loud, cheesy, and proudly Texan, precisely what people came there for.

Jerry picked up one of the arcade pistols on the counter, its steel frame cold and unexpectedly heavy for something meant to entertain tourists. He wrapped his fingers around the grip, feeling the smooth wear from countless hands before his. It wasn't a real gun, but the weight fooled his muscles into recalling the real ones, memories he'd worked hard to drown. Jerry was reminded that he lost his right to own a gun after his felony conviction.

He then thought about how Control had given him a second chance. The man was a bit of a mystery, but one thing that Control would not let him do was wallow in pity. Control demanded high standards from his agents. Jerry had practiced for hours at the PROACTIVE training ranges, honing his skills.

He inserted a few tokens into the machine. Lights flickered on, and the desert scenery buzzed into life. Jerry raised the pistol, testing the trigger. It had that cheap, springy resistance, but there was a moment, his mind filled in the blanks with the memory of recoil, smoke, and the sharp punch of a real shot.

He aimed at an outlaw, exhaled, and squeezed the trigger. The pistol clicked sharply, and the silhouette spun backward with a satisfying clang. Something eased in him. Not joy, just familiarity. He fired again. Another outlaw fell. Then another. He settled into a rhythm, and the arcade faded away around him. For a moment, he wasn't in a tourist trap. He was back in the Old West his imagination had clung to since he was a kid, where the lines between good men and bad men were supposed to be clear. Gunslingers faced off under blazing skies, heroes stood proud, and villains showed their true intentions plain as day.

But life hadn't stayed that simple. Not for him. In the real world, the good guys and bad guys wore the same boots, rode the same roads, and sometimes lived in the same skin.

He fired at a rattlesnake target. Hit it dead center. The tin serpent flopped over with a mechanical hiss, and the arcade's tiny saloon piano sprang to life, playing a shaky tune as if congratulating him. Jerry didn't feel congratulated. The shots were too easy. Too natural. As if the Old West he imagined, clean, moral, storybook, had never existed at all.

He lowered the pistol and stared at it for a long moment. It wasn't real, but his hands didn't seem to know the difference. He checked his watch. His table should be ready in five minutes. Jerry put the pistol down and went to get his table.

As Jerry was shown to his table. While hundreds of miles to the west, Johnny parked his motorcycle behind a nondescript building in an industrial park north of Tucson.

He walked up to the back door and punched in a code on the keypad. A clicking sound was heard as the door unlocked. Once inside, he walked down a narrow hallway. The walls were painted white, the floor hard, polished concrete, clean enough to reflect the overhead fluorescent lights that hummed softly and cast a cool, even glow. The air smelled faintly of disinfectants, mixed with something metallic or chemical that was hard to place.

There was only one door at the end, with a sign reading Authorized Personnel Only. Johnny went through it as if he belonged there. Once inside, he saw a locker room. One locker was specifically for him. He opened it and began to change.

After a few moments, Johnny was transformed. Layers of protective gear almost entirely erased his identity. The white bio suit covered him from neck to ankle, slightly loose but cinched at the wrists and waist, its smooth, synthetic fabric faintly crinkling with every movement. The suit reflected the light cleanly, giving him a stark, almost clinical silhouette.

He wore a full-face respirator mask on his head, the clear visor hiding his facial features behind a curved sheen of glass and plastic. Filters protruded from the sides, giving the mask a bulky, industrial look. Behind the visor, his eyes were visible but distant, magnified slightly. His breathing came out as a steady, filtered hiss and soft whoosh, mechanical and close, punctuated by the faint flutter of the respirator's valves.

On Ringo's hands were black nitrile gloves stretching over his fingers so precisely that every movement looked deliberate and careful. His boots were wrapped in disposable booties, the material gathered and elasticized around his ankles, muting the sound of his footsteps. A hair covering fit snugly over his head, ensuring not a single strand could escape.

Johnny stood in front of a full-length mirror for one last visual inspection. Satisfied, he turned away and headed for the only other door at the opposite end of the room. He entered another code, and the lock clicked open with a soft hiss as the pressure seal lifted. With his right hand, he pulled the door open.

At first, he was surprised by how heavy the door was. Then he remembered it was heavier because it was the inner laboratory door.

Once he was inside, he pushed the door closed until he heard the lock click. Johnny looked around as he stood at the front of the lab and saw a room boxed in by strict dimensions, forty feet by forty feet, with a ceiling fifteen feet high that contained a state-of-the-art filtration system. The only sounds were the faint thrum of fans blowing and the quiet gurgle of water from some of the flasks on the workbenches.

Straight rows of workbenches stretched away from him, their scarred surfaces holding many different-shaped flasks made of Pyrex. Some were round at the bottom, others flat and tapered. A few sat above unlit burners. There were two flasks on lit burners, their contents bubbling. A few had cork seals.

Most were empty, some were filled with various shades of red or blue liquid. The overhead lights cast a flat, unforgiving glow that erased shadows rather than creating them, making every object feel exposed and deliberate. There were three others inside the lab dressed like Johnny.

One was working under one of the fume hoods that lined the walls. His name was Deepak. Johnny could not see exactly what the man was doing. A second man was working at a computer next to a stack of metal boxes. His name was Adesh.

Johnny knew exactly what Adesh was sitting next to. It was a High-Performance Liquid Chromatograph. Also called an HPLC, it was a boxy, bench-top instrument made of stacked modules connected by thin tubing, with solvent bottles on top and a small column tucked inside the flow path. It ran quietly while a nearby computer displayed sharp peaks representing the sample's components, and the results appeared as simple lines and peaks on the screen. The machine was often used to determine the concentration of certain drugs.

Finally, Bibek was the name of the third man to his right, who was using a pipette to extract a reddish substance into a test tube. A faint chemical sharpness hung in the air, stale and persistent, and beneath it all lay a heavy stillness.

Johnny knew these men. He hired them for this special project. They were three Indian chemical engineers currently in the United States on H-1B visas. They technically worked for him, but not directly.

An H-1B visa is a U.S. work visa that permits employers to temporarily hire foreign professionals in specialized fields that typically require at least a bachelor's degree or its equivalent. It is commonly used in sectors such as technology, engineering, science, and medicine, and is employer-sponsored, meaning the worker can work only for the sponsoring company.

Another company in Tucson had actually hired them. Johnny had offered them an opportunity to make some extra money on the side and they gladly agreed.

Johnny watched as Bibek filled a test tube and put it in a desktop centrifuge. He hit a switch, and the machine started with a low electric whir that quickly rose into a smooth, steady hum as it spun up to speed. After a moment, it slowed. The man lifted the test tube and observed the contents.

Johnny stepped toward Bibek.

"Is it ready?" Johnny asked. His voice muffled and slightly distorted, filtered through the respirator into a flat, enclosed tone with a faint echo and the soft hiss of air riding beneath his words.

Bibek turned to him. His eyes gave Johnny the impression that he was smiling, if only he could see his mouth.

Bibek nodded. "Yes."

He had the same muffled tone as Johnny.

Then Bibek turned and walked across the room to Adesh sitting at the computer. Johnny followed as he listened to the sound of his own breathing. He seemed to be breathing heavier than usual. Maybe it was the anticipation of this being the finished product.

Bibek stopped at the HPLC and loaded the liquid into the machine. He pressed some buttons and waited. After a few moments, Adesh typed a few lines and hit enter. The man turned around in his chair and clapped his hands.

"The formula is complete, and it is being transferred to a portable drive," the man said in a muffled voice. Even with his mask on, Johnny could hear the man's heavy accent.

Johnny nodded with approval. "Applications?"

Bibek answered, "Aerosol, liquid, surface application, such as coating or films, gas, and vapor if it is heated, and finally direct ingestion."

"What about absorptive contact?" Johnny asked.

"No. The easiest ways are inhalation, ingestion, or injection," Bibek explained.

Johnny grinned under his mask as he thought.

Colt's destruction is at hand.

"Excellent. How much of the product do you have ready?" Johnny asked.

"A liter. We have it ready for you. One moment, please," Bibek said.

Bibek walked over to Deepak, and there was a brief conversation that Johnny didn't understand. Deepak put down what he was doing and closed the door to the hood chamber. He reached under his table and handed Bibek a black Pelican case, a little larger than a briefcase.

Coming over to Johnny, Bibek placed it on the center workbench and stepped back. Johnny walked forward, pressed the pressure-release button on the case, and thumbed the two side locks. They clicked open.

Johnny then opened the case and looked inside. What he saw were forty 25 ml tubes neatly stacked in racks, with black foam inserts between them to protect them.

He picked one up and held it to the light. The crimson-colored liquid inside caught it immediately, glowing a vivid, unsettling red.

"Ah, Johnny Reb, my opus pulchrum! You synthetic beautiful bastard."

"I am sorry, my English isn't always that good. Could you repeat, please?" Bibek asked.

Still holding the tube up to the light, he looked over his shoulder at Bibek.

"Opus pulchrum means a beautiful work in classical Latin."

"Thank you," Bibek said.

Johnny put the tube back in its place and carefully closed and locked the case. All three of the men were standing together now. Adesh handed Johnny a small black case no larger than a deck of cards.

"Here is the only copy. So, don't lose it," the man said with a laugh.

"I'll make sure not to. I will have your payments brought here to you in two hours," Johnny said, picking up the case.

"Thank you," the trio said in unison.

Johnny left the same way he came in. Once back in his biker attire, he walked out and put the black case in one of his saddlebags. He slid out his phone and dialed.

"Yes," a woman answered in a soft, husky voice.

"All right, darling, time for payment," Johnny said.

"Understood," the woman answered and hung up the phone.

Johnny started his bike and roared off into the night. His thoughts went back to the days when he had another name, the old stuffy name of Reginald Prescott, third heir to Prescott Chemical and Pharmaceuticals. He was raised in the best private schools, taught classical Latin by a tutor because his mother demanded it. He was being groomed to take over someday, when everyone finally died.

He had spent his weekends working in the labs to develop a new money-making wonder drug. Reginald became disillusioned as he entered college. Wasn't there more to life than this? Where was the risk? Where was the excitement?

He and some friends watched the 1993 version of Tombstone in his private theater at home, during an Old West-themed party. The movie changed him. He was not a fan of the Earps, far from it, or idealized Doc Holiday. Reginald was drawn to Johnny Ringo. There was just something about the character.

He began to read everything he could get his hands on about Ringo, which wasn't much. Reginald even went to a Medium to try to make contact with Ringo's spirit. One woman convinced him after they had intercourse that she felt the spirit of Johnny Ringo in him as they made love.

Reginald finished college and dutifully started working for the family. At twenty-five, he faced a choice. Either take a lump-sum inheritance and be cut off forever from the family or take a seat on the company board.

To the family's shock, he took the lump sum. No one in the family's history had ever taken it before. His mother fainted, and his father stormed out. His siblings thought he was joking. The family ordered a psychological evaluation of Reginald. The diagnosis came back that he was normal. The actual diagnosis was that he was a sociopath, but he had paid the psychiatrist twice what his parents had for the evaluation.

Reginald held firm and took his money. He then legally changed his name and headed west to Arizona. This turned out to be a rather fortuitous choice for Reginald. Within a year of his departure, several class action lawsuits were filed, and it was found that there had been some bad batches of their pharmaceuticals released that resulted in death. Then the Federal government came after the company from every angle. EPA, FBI, FDA, you name it.

It was rumored that someone had tipped off the lawyers and the government, someone who was very well placed. Reginald's father decided the only honorable thing was to commit a murder-suicide with his wife. His brother was left holding the bag. Once everything was over, there was nothing left except a large Class A motor home, which the bankruptcy judge allowed his brother to keep because, under bankruptcy law, it was his house and only means of transportation.

Johnny didn't care. They had made their choices, and he had made his. He was no longer a trust-fund baby. Reginald Prescott was dead. Johnny Ringo was alive and doing quite well, just like the legends of the Old West. This Johnny was going to make a name for himself.

CHAPTER 7

Back in Texas, Jerry had finished his steak, rode the shuttle back to the RV park, and was in his Conestoga. His body was tired, but his brain was still awake. He wanted something to calm him so he could sleep. Jerry found the television remote. He flipped through some channels. Finding nothing interesting, he turned it off.

His brain was still wide awake. He thought maybe something to read would help his insomnia. Jerry went to the office. He had seen a bookshelf earlier. Perhaps they had something he could read. The office was about to close as he came in. The young woman was closing the office when the doorbell rang as Jerry came in.

"We're closed," the woman said from another room.

"I'm just looking for something to read," Jerry said.

"Take anything from the bookshelf but make it quick. You can keep it," the woman responded.

Jerry got the message and went to the bookshelf. The first book he found was titled The Bird Cage Theater: *The Curtain Rises on Tombstone, Arizona's National Treasure*. He flipped it over in his hand and read the back cover, nodded in approval, and headed for the door with the book in hand.

"Thank you," Jerry shouted as he left the office.

"You're welcome," came the reply.

The doorbell rang as he left. After a moment, he was back in his room, lying on the bed, reading the book. Slowly, his eyes closed, the book sliding from his fingers as he drifted off to sleep.

While Jerry was in his first REM sleep cycle, two men were drinking beer and sitting at a table outside a bar in Tucson.

The first man was named Jeffery Banks. He was tall and broad-shouldered. He wore a plain blue denim cut over a faded black T-shirt. The denim vest had no large back patch, no decoration, just a small "PROSPECT" identifier on the front. His jeans were dark and straight-leg, tucked slightly into worn black leather boots that showed scuffs from riding.

The second man was named Larry Sellers, a bit shorter and leaner, built like someone who rode hard and often. He wore a black leather cut, equally unadorned except for the same identifier as his friend, over a long-sleeved black shirt. The leather was broken-in, creased at the shoulders and edges, suggesting time on the road. His jeans were clean but utilitarian, held up with a plain belt.

Bank's phone buzzed, he pulled it out and looked at the screen, the words "Not Listed" were on the screen.

He pressed the answer button.

"Yes?" he said.

"Ready to earn your colors, prospect?" a husky female asked.

Banks suddenly sat up straight. Sellers stared at Banks.

"Yes, I am."

"Who's with you?" the woman asked.

Banks raised his eyebrows as he looked over at Sellers.

"Sellers."

"Good." Her voice was smooth and silky.

"Bring him with you. The club needs you to make a delivery. Go to the warehouse, follow the instructions there to the letter. You will leave your bikes, absolutely no club markings. Do you understand?" she said.

"Yes, yes, I do," Banks said.

"You two have been loyal. Once you do this, you'll earn your colors," the voice said.

The line went dead. Banks looked at the phone and then at Sellers.

"Bro, it was her. We need to go to the warehouse. She said that if we do this, we will get our colors."

The two men fist-pumped and downed their beers. They stood up and mounted their motorcycles. The pair started their motorcycles and roared off into the night.

An hour later, Banks and Sellers were wearing blue jumpsuits and tennis shoes, driving a white, windowless delivery van. They pulled into the back parking lot where Johnny had parked earlier.

They backed up to the door. Banks parked, and they both got out. Sellers picked up a duffel bag as he got out. Banks punched numbers into the keypad to open the door. They walked down the hall into the locker room. Deepak, Adesh, and Bibek, now in street clothes, were surprised when the two men entered the room.

"We are here to take you back. The gift is in the truck," Banks said.

The three men smiled.

"Thank you," Bibek said in a heavy accent.

"I need one of you to open the lab," Sellers said.

Deepak said nothing and opened the lab door.

"Wait here and keep the door open," Sellers said as he went inside.

He set the duffel bag on the floor and opened it. A digital clock was attached to blocks of C4 explosives. He set the timer for sixty minutes and pressed the button. The timer started counting down. He stood up and left the room.

"You can close the door now," Sellers said as he passed Deepak.

Deepak nodded and closed the door.

"Let's go," Banks said.

He turned and left. Sellers and the three engineers followed. Once outside, Banks went up and got into the driver's seat. Sellers opened the van's back doors, and the three engineers climbed inside. The three men got into the van and sat on the bench seats along the sides. The floor was flat, with no foot wells, so their shoes rested directly on the metal as they faced each other across the open space. Sellers slammed the doors closed and joined Banks up front in the passenger seat.

Banks started the van and drove out of the parking lot. He headed east out to the desert.

"We are meeting out in the desert," Banks said over his shoulder.

Banks drove the van steadily down East Tanque Verde Road through a quiet Tucson neighborhood, passing low stucco houses and darkened yards beneath a sky scattered with stars. As streetlights thinned, the homes fell away, and the van turned onto Redington Road, a long, empty road leading toward the desert.

The pavement hummed beneath the tires until it ended at a cattle guard, the metal bars clanking as the van crossed. Beyond it, the road became dirt, dust lifting faintly in the headlights. With no moon overhead and only the darkness pressing in, the van slowed and came to a stop in a small, unlit parking lot of the Upper Tanque Verde Trailhead. The lot was deserted at this hour.

About half a mile farther up Reddington Road, a curvaceous woman with strong, expressive features sat still in the darkness, a small knapsack at her side.

Her Spanish heritage was evident in her thick, long, dark hair, loosely pulled back at the nape of her neck. Most would consider her petite, standing just five feet four inches. She had a prominent brow and calm, hazel eyes that missed very little. Her face appeared sharply in the starlight with high cheekbones and full lips set in a neutral, patient line. Her appearance let her get away with a lot that most people can't. Her name was Lucia Santiago.

She wore dark, practical clothing meant to disappear into the desert night: a fitted black jacket, dusty boots, and jeans dulled by use. A lightweight scarf was wrapped once around her neck. She blended easily with the rocks and scrub around her, seated low and steady, posture relaxed but alert.

At night in July, the Tucson desert still held the day's heat, radiating warmth from rocks and sand even after sunset. The air was heavy and still, with the distant smell of creosote from recent monsoon rain. Cacti stood as dark silhouettes against a star-crowded sky, and the quiet was broken only by insects and a slight wind. There was a far-off rumble of thunder on the horizon.

Lucia raised a pair of infrared binoculars and looked down toward the Upper Tanque Verde Trailhead. Through the lenses, the world shifted into a palette of glowing white and gray. The desert floor radiated faint heat, brush and rocks outlined like ghosts. The parking lot appeared as a pale rectangle against the cooler ground.

She watched the van arrive, its engine heat blooming brightly as it slowed. The tires rolled in, the vehicle turned, and then stopped. The engine cut off, leaving a lingering glow that slowly faded. No other movement followed—no doors opening yet, no figures stepping out. She held the binoculars steady, observing in silence, committing the moment to memory while the desert remained otherwise still.

Lucia looked around for a watchful eye. Finding none, she pulled out her phone from inside her jacket and turned it on. The screen's glow illuminated her face as she dialed a number.

"Yes," Johnny said.

"Your package has arrived," she said in a husky voice.

"Good. I have some business up north. When I'm done, I'll call you," he said.

"Don't be too long. You wouldn't want my fire to go out," she said seductively.

"Oh, you know I wouldn't let that happen. Now, you might want to put your head down," Johnny said, and hung up.

Lucia looked down as she put the phone back into her jacket.

Down at the parking lot, Banks opened the driver's door.

"I've got to take a leak," Banks said over his shoulder to everyone.

He stepped out of the van and slammed the door as he walked to the back. Just as he unzipped his fly, he saw a bright white flash, and that would be the last thing he would ever see.

A sudden flash tore through the night, turning darkness into blinding white for an instant. A deep, rolling shock followed that echoed off the surrounding hills, and a column of fire and smoke surged upward, billowing and folding in on itself. As it climbed, the plume spread wide at the top, forming a towering mushroom cloud that glowed faintly before dissolving into drifting ash and shadow.

Lucia saw the flash of the explosion light up the ground. Then she waited for the sound.

Nothing came.

The blast wave raced outward at ground level, but the ridge and the colder air above it bent the sound away. The sound lifted, slid, and broke apart as it traveled, passing over her position rather than reaching it. She sat in what is called an acoustic dead zone, a thin pocket of quiet created by terrain and air working against the wave.

She didn't hear the sound that came down in waves, as scattered metallic rain clattered against dirt and rock. Smaller fragments hissed and snapped as they struck the ground, while heavier pieces of the engine landed with dull, hollow thuds that echoed briefly in the open desert. Then there was a fading patter of loose debris settling. An enormous crater, filled with debris, was all that remained of the van and its occupants. She did one last scan with her binoculars to see if anyone had survived. Satisfied, she picked up her knapsack, brushed the dirt off her bottom, and began to hike away, disappearing into the night.

The explosion stirred memories in Lucia of the violence she had witnessed as a child. She was born in Juárez, Mexico, the daughter of Rosa Santiago, a nightclub singer once kept by a cartel lieutenant. Her mother's charm was her curse, adored, used, and discarded by the man who owned her. Lucia was born addicted to the drugs her mother used to survive, a sickly child who was told early she could never bear children.

Rosa called her *mi fuego pequeño*, *my little fire*, for the fierce will in her eyes even as a baby. When she was sixteen, her mother vanished, either killed or taken, no one ever knew. Lucía was left to fend for herself in a world where her beauty became her currency. She had been blessed with her mother's voice and her talent for singing. She began singing in the same kind of clubs her mother had died in. Just like her mother, she caught the eye of a cartel member.

Lucia had no intention of ending up like her mother, so she fled to the

United States. Lucia told them she had left a cartel leader and that his people had already tried to kill her. She showed messages, names, and dates, and explained why the police back home could not protect her. That was enough to establish credible fear.

Once U.S. Citizenship and Immigration Services officers confirmed the threats were real and ongoing, returning her was no longer an option. The government had a duty not to send someone back to be executed. When it became clear she also understood how the cartel operated and who was involved, her case was flagged as high-risk and urgent.

Lucia's interviews were scheduled back-to-back, paperwork was moved without sitting for months, and decisions were made quickly. She was not granted asylum as a reward, but her cooperation mattered. It showed she was acting in good faith, and it gave the government reason to move her to the front of the line and protect her.

She lay low in Texas for the eight years it took to obtain her citizenship. In that time, the man who had sought to possess her had died at the hands of another cartel. Once she became a citizen, she moved to Arizona to start a new life.

That's where Johnny Ringo found her, or she found him. She was performing at a private party in Tucson, Arizona. He caught her after her set, smiling like he already knew her. He was charming and handsome in his white dinner jacket, black pants, and bow-tied tuxedo shirt. She felt an immediate attraction for him.

He told her she had a rare voice, not just good but memorable, and said it with total confidence, as if stating a fact. He was calm, self-assured, and confident. She had ended up going home with him. That was five years ago.

But something had changed. He became self-obsessed with his motorcycle gang. Over time, he had made it clear that she was his woman, and he would not tolerate any competition. He hadn't been violent to her, but she noticed that a waiter at a restaurant they frequented had quit after having a bad accident in the parking lot.

After striking a deal with Frank Colt for access to his routes for something Johnny called a "toll tax," he had become increasingly paranoid. She couldn't figure out why.

He had never physically abused her, quite the opposite, but she knew it would only be a matter of time. Johnny was becoming just like the cartel man she had fled.

As Lucia hiked over another hill, she was too far away to hear or see the laboratory explode. Tucson's finest would be busy tonight.

CHAPTER 8

The next morning in Amarillo, a strong gust of wind shook the Conestoga. Jerry woke up with a start. Another wind gust shook the wagon again. It took him a moment to get his bearings. He swung his legs over the side of the bed and rubbed his face. His face contorted in annoyance as he realized he had slept in his clothes.

Jerry made a wide yawn, stood, and stretched. He checked the time on his phone. It was seven thirty.

I'm burning daylight, Jerry thought.

He quickly stepped outside to grab a clean T-shirt. He noticed the sky was overcast. Jerry went back inside to wash up and change. Once that was completed, he headed to the office to check out.

By the time he stepped into the office at Big Tex RV Park, his jacket was zipped and his skull cap on. The same pretty clerk was behind the counter. Jerry told her he was checking out.

"Where are you headin'?" she asked with a smooth Texas drawl.

"North, to Oklahoma, Colorado, Nebraska, then on into the Badlands."

She got quiet and pointed to the large TV mounted on the wall. A weather radar bloomed across the screen in reds and yellows, a storm system already moving east and curling north.

"That's coming your way," she said. "Sooner than later."

Jerry watched the screen for a second, then nodded. Outside, the wind pressed harder against the building, and the light had begun to drain from the day.

"I've got an appointment to make," Jerry said.

"Appointments don't mean anything if you're dead. You're about to ride right through tornado alley. Do you at least have a helmet to keep your handsome noggin in one piece?" she said.

"Yes, I do." He signed out and headed for the door.

He looked at the darkening sky as he started his bike. He was about to pop the kickstand when the woman's words came back to him.

What kind of sponsor am I if I don't live by my own words? Am I letting this ride become an addiction?

He got off the bike, pulled the helmet from the saddlebag, and put it on. He adjusted the chin strap, got back on his motorcycle, flipped up the visor, and popped the kickstand. Jerry turned the throttle slightly as the rumble of the bike's engines echoed off the wooden fence, and he rode to the exit. Once at the exit, he checked the traffic and roared off.

Maybe I can beat the rain, or better still, it keeps ahead of me, Jerry thought as he rode.

He would ride north on U.S. 287 for most of the way, through the Oklahoma panhandle, then through the Front Range of Colorado. Once Jerry crossed I-76, he would turn slightly east, cross Nebraska, and finally end up in the Badlands. The total ride would be about ten hours after leaving Amarillo. Jerry thought he could make it if the weather held.

Two hours outside of Amarillo, he was riding through Boise City, Oklahoma. The sky was still overcast, but no rain fell. There was an occasional heavy gust of wind across the road, but it was not strong enough to make Jerry abandon his goal.

Fifteen minutes later, Jerry crossed the Oklahoma/Colorado border. He looked down at his fuel gauge. He was running low on gas. Jerry saw a road sign that let him know Campo Colorado was only about ten minutes away. He had enough gas to make it to the town.

A grain elevator rose above everything else, pale and utilitarian, visible long before the town came into view. A few minutes later, Campo came into view under a sky that hadn't made up its mind yet. Jerry saw the storm getting closer. Not close enough to touch, but close enough to feel. The air had cooled, and the wind carried the smell of ozone and rain.

The short grass shivered in uneven waves, and dust lifted from the shoulders of the road, drifting east. Fence posts stood out sharply against the sky, and the horizon felt closer than it should, as if the weather was pressing it inward. Far off, beneath a thick band of cloud, Jerry could see rain falling, dark streaks sliding across the land.

Still miles away, Jerry thought.

Campo itself sat quietly and unchanged, a handful of buildings clustered near the road, and the windows reflected the sky. The town gave off the feeling of being forged by hard work and sweat. It was connected by the Santa Fe Trail and by its proximity to the Comanche National Grasslands. Interestingly, Campo is often cited as one of Colorado's most isolated towns.

For people traveling in southeastern Colorado, especially along Highway 287 or nearby routes, Campo is known as a fuel-and-coffee stop, not a destination. Clarence's Truck Stop is emblematic of that role.

Jerry slowed and turned into Clarence's Truck Stop. He eased the bike to a stop by the pump and cut the engine. He took off his helmet and noticed that the sudden silence made the wind more noticeable, as it tugged at his jacket and hummed through power lines.

He filled the tank, keeping one eye on the west. The clouds were stacking higher now, their undersides darkening. The edge of the storm was drawing closer. Thunder muttered somewhere far off, low, not yet a threat, just a warning. The light kept thinning, turning the prairie a dull gold and gray.

Jerry went into the truck stop, bought a bottle of water, and paid for his gas. He finished his water and threw the empty bottle into the trash. He put his helmet back on and started his bike.

Jerry eased the bike back onto the road, continuing his quest north. He was careful to obey the town's speed limit. Finally, he made it to the edge of town. Jerry increased his speed as the town slipped behind him and the prairie opened up again, uninterrupted. The grain elevator faded in his mirrors, then disappeared entirely. The road stretched on, straight and patient, and the motorcycle settled back into its steady rhythm. Campo was already gone, leaving only the sense that he passed through somewhere honest, even if it barely marked the map.

Jerry kept riding north on U.S. 287 with the steady, deliberate posture the Fat Boy seemed to demand. The Harley's low, solid weight was a comfort. It seemed to be unmoved by the crosswind that blew down from the Front Range. Mid-morning light lay flat across the plains, not bright so much as exposed, as if the day hadn't decided what it wanted to be yet.

The sky to the west was darkening by degrees. Not dramatic, not suddenly, just a slow thickening of gray, like a bruise forming. Light filtered through the clouds in dull sheets, flattening the land and draining color from the fields. He could feel the change before the rain arrived. The temperature dropped, the air sharpened, and then came the smell of dust and ozone.

A feeling of disappointment came over Jerry that he might not make it to the Badlands today. He unconsciously gunned the throttle.

I can't let Mark down. He's depending on me, Jerry thought.

Ahead of him, a curtain of rain was already falling, and a slanted gray veil moved across the road. He watched it advance, measuring distance the way riders do, how long until it reached him, how hard it looked, whether it might break apart. It didn't. It kept coming, steady and wide, swallowing the highway a mile at a time.

The few cars and trucks that passed had their headlights on, as drivers do after being in a rainstorm. Each one pushed a brief wall of wind against him. Jerry stayed loose on the bars, letting the bike do what it was built to do. The engine's rhythm carried up through the seat and into his legs, grounding him. Riding always narrowed his thoughts.

Just outside Kit Carson, the storm arrived without ceremony. The first drops hit his helmet hard enough to sound like gravel. Rain darkened the leather of his gloves and streaked the tank. Within seconds, it was coming down in bands, thick sheets that slapped his jacket and soaked through the seams. Water drummed on his helmet and ran down the inside of his collar. Visibility shrank.

The road blurred into a gray tunnel.

This could go really bad, quick, thought Jerry.

He knew that if he lost control and had to lay the bike down, he was no match for a seven-hundred-pound piece of steel and chrome. That is, if he didn't have any other type of accident, like someone pulling out in front of him or losing control and ending up in a ditch.

Jerry didn't push it. He rolled off the throttle and scanned for shelter. The Kit Carson Inn appeared through the rain, low, squat, a place meant to wait things out. He turned in, boots skidding slightly on wet pavement, and coasted under the overhang. When he shut the bike down, the rain seemed to roar overhead. The wind blew the rain sideways at him.

Inside, Jerry took off his helmet and held it in his hand. He left a trail of water across the floor. The clerk looked up from the counter and took him in, wet jacket, road grit on his jeans, helmet tucked under his arm. The look wasn't hostile, just wary, as if the storm had blown something unexpected through the door.

The clerk was in his late middle age, lean in a way that comes from habit rather than exercise. His thinning hair was cut short, more practical than styled, with gray working in at the temples. He wore wire-rim glasses that sat low on his nose, and he looked over them instead of through them when someone walked in. He had a narrow, weathered face, the skin darkened by the sun, even though he spent most of his day indoors.

He was plainly dressed, in a faded button-down shirt, tucked into his faded blue jeans. The sleeves were rolled just enough to show his forearms marked by old scars and sun. There was a pen clipped in his shirt pocket.

"Storm caught you," the clerk said, more statement than question.

Jerry grinned. "You might say that."

He set his helmet down. Outside, rain hammered the windows, and the sky continued to darken.

"I was hoping you had a room?" Jerry asked.

He stood there dripping, listening to the weather, feeling the ride still humming in his bones.

The clerk made no expression.

"You're in luck. We have a few. Cash or card?" the clerk asked.

"How much?"

The clerk looked at Jerry for a moment. Jerry wasn't sure whether the man was sizing him up or making a judgment call about whether to rent to him.

"How long?"

"One night," Jerry said.

"Eighty dollars," the man replied.

Jerry reached into his front pocket and pulled out some money. He counted out eighty soggy dollars and gave them to the man.

"Sorry," Jerry said with a sheepish grin.

The man said nothing as he put the money into a drawer under the desk. He pulled out a piece of paper and a room key, placing them on the counter.

The man pointed to the paper. "Standard stuff. You break it, you buy it. Initial here, here, and here, then sign at the bottom."

Jerry did as he was told and took the key. "Thanks."

The man just nodded. Jerry turned and went back outside. The rain had subsided slightly. There was a bright flash of lightning. Jerry counted the seconds until the thunderclap. Sixteen seconds.

Out on the plains, the counting becomes more than a rule of thumb. It's a way of measuring scale. Five seconds might mean a localized cell, something that will pass off to the side. Fifteen or twenty seconds means something bigger, wider, a storm that owns a lot of sky. He knew the storm wasn't even close to being over.

He started his bike and parked it parallel to his room, under the awning in front of it. Jerry didn't think anyone was going to tell him to move it in this storm. He quickly opened the door and then went back out to unload his saddlebags. Jerry thought nothing was worse than riding in wet clothes. He made it in before the next wave of rain came, and flipped the switch on the wall to turn on the room's lights.

The room was functional and straightforward. A double bed with a dark brown bedspread sat against the wall, neatly made with folded towels placed on top. The floor was light wood-colored laminate, clean and bare. Opposite the bed stood a small dresser with a microwave and a mini-fridge beneath it, and a flat-screen TV mounted on the wall above. There was a vanity sink at the far end of the room, and a door leading to a shower and a commode. Overall, it felt like a modest roadside motel room, plain, tidy, and meant more for rest than comfort.

The rain pounded on the roof, and the thunder increased.

Jerry set the helmet and phone on top of the dresser, then picked up the TV remote. He turned on the television and scrolled through the channels. He found a station that played reruns of shows from the sixties. *The Rifleman* was playing. It was a classic Western about a widowed rancher who raises his son while defending justice in a rough frontier town.

"Ha!" Jerry laughed out loud.

The show had been in rerun before Jerry was born. He liked these shows because they portrayed dignity, structure, and the idea that a man is more than his past. A message that mattered a lot to Jerry, who had lived on the margins. Maybe that was the deeper reason he joined PROACTIVE.

Jerry threw the control on the bed and stripped down to his underwear. He hung his jacket up and his pants and shirt over the shower curtain rod. He got a towel and laid it on the floor beneath his jacket.

He picked up his phone and dialed his friend Mark.

"Hello," Mark's voice echoed.

"Hey, man. This connection is awful," Jerry almost yelled his response.

The rain poured down, and there was a thunderclap. Jerry heard a crackle of electricity come over the connection.

"I guess you got caught in a storm. The weather's great here in Deadwood,"

Mark said.

"Yeah, and it's pretty bad. I'm going to be a little late. I won't be able to get there until at least tomorrow," Jerry said.

"No worries, man. It can wait one more day," Mark's voice echoed.

"Thanks, I'd better get off the phone," Jerry said.

"See you tomorrow night. It will be the same place that I sent you before, be safe," Mark said.

"I will, bro," Jerry said.

"Ok, bye," Mark said and hung up the phone.

Jerry set the phone on the dresser, picked up the TV remote, and lay down on the bed. Just as he was turning up the volume, the power went out. The room went dark. Jerry sighed.

The storm raged outside. The floor lit up as flashes of lightning flickered through the space under the room door. Jerry noticed how quiet the room was, no sound from the fridge or the air conditioner, just silence, except for the rain outside.

He thought about all those background noises that people ignore. Jerry cocked his arm under his head as he stared at the darkened ceiling. For a moment, he was back in his prison cell. The rain and thunder morphed into the noises of metal doors rolling shut. Voices yelling somewhere. He shook his head and came back to the present.

The storm was starting to subside a bit. The power was still out. Jerry didn't think the place had a backup generator. He would have to wait it out. Jerry sighed, then got up again, pulled back the covers, and climbed in. He figured he would try to get some sleep. He rolled over and pulled one of the pillows over his head to block the noise of the storm. Surprisingly, he fell asleep.

CHAPTER 9

Jerry woke with a start as the power came back on, the television displayed the message "No Signal" on the screen. Jerry sat up and got his bearings. There was a low hum as the refrigerator's compressor came on. He stretched, got out of bed, and headed to the bathroom. He checked the time on his phone. It was 5 a.m. Jerry took his now-dry clothes from the curtain rod and threw them onto the bed. He got ready to shower and closed the door.

An hour later, after Jerry showered and dressed, he was headed north on County Road 20. He rode with helmet visor up. The sun was up, and the sky was a vivid blue. The sun made the colors of the Eastern Plains of Colorado look like something out of a Norman Rockwell painting. There wasn't a cloud in the sky. Roadside puddles mirrored the blue sky. Jerry smiled as he looked around. Ahead of him, the gray-black strip of road stretched off to the horizon.

What a beautiful day, he thought.

Jerry breathed in the fresh, clean air. He felt so alive, so free. There wasn't a car or truck in either direction for miles. The only sound was the wind passing and the bike's low rumble. He would be in the Badlands in about seven hours. This was going to be a great day. He felt as if the storm had washed the land clean, and somehow his soul.

He gave the throttle a slight twist, and the bike responded with a slow, confident surge. The scenery flew by, and a feeling of exhilaration flowed through him.

Two and a half hours later, he stopped for gas in Peetz, Colorado, and twenty minutes later crossed the Nebraska border. He had checked his directions on his phone and knew he had another three and a half hours to go before he hit the South Dakota border. Jerry thought he was making great time. He thought he might even have time to detour to see Mount Rushmore. He would check at the South Dakota state line.

Jerry rode north across western Nebraska. The mid-July sun was high, and the land spread out wide and unhurried around him. The prairie rolled just enough to keep the horizon moving, grass and pasture broken by fence lines, grain elevators, and the occasional water tower marking a town he'd pass through without stopping. Heat pressed in whenever he slowed, easing only at speed, the air was warm and heavy against his jacket.

He smelled dry grass, dust, and cattle on the wind, with brief hints of damp earth near irrigated fields. The engine's steady drone and the rush of wind filled his helmet, interrupted now and then by a passing pickup or the snap of insects against his visor. Miles went by without drama. The road was patient and straight, as Jerry kept heading north, small against the scale of the plains but moving steadily through them.

Jerry stopped in Pine Ridge at the Nebraska line and did the math in his head. There was plenty of daylight left, he fueled the tank, and nothing was slowing him down. He made his decision. Yes, he would take the detour and see Mount Rushmore.

He crossed into South Dakota, and the ride changed fast. The road started to rise and bend, grass giving way to pine and rock. The air cooled a notch and smelled sharper. Traffic picked up, tourists in rental cars, RVs drifting wide in the curves, and more motorcycles, pairs and small packs, all headed the same direction. Nobody waved much. They didn't need to. The town of Keystone came at him loud and tight, gift shops stacked on both sides, Harleys idling at the curb, chrome and leather and engines popping in the heat. He rolled through slowly, feeling out of place and exactly where he was supposed to be, the hills closing in like they had a point to make.

By the time he reached Mount Rushmore, the road narrowed, and the trees opened just enough. The faces hit him all at once, bigger than photos, heavier somehow, staring past him instead of at him. He shut the bike off, and the silence rang in his ears. Other bikers parked nearby, helmets off, nobody talking much. Jerry stood there thinking about the miles behind him, the flat nothing of Nebraska, the way the road had folded up into rock and history without asking his opinion. The monument didn't move him patriotically, but he could definitely see how people could be. Standing before the massive faces made him feel small and temporary, like the ride itself, passing through something that would still be there long after he was gone. The sun was getting lower in the sky. He didn't stay long. Jerry had an appointment to make.

The sun was sliding down behind the Black Hills, turning Deadwood the color of old brass. On the main street of the historic district, Johnny Ringo sat back in his chair outside Mustang Sally's Bar and Grill, boots hooked on the rail.

Two of his boys flanked him, Jimmy on the left, twitchy fingers never far from his cigarette, and Dale on the right, built like a hitching post and just as expressive. The three men wore no colors on their backs, no rockers to announce who they were, but it didn't matter. They wanted to stay low-key without disappearing. Heads still turned, glances still lingered. Johnny liked being seen.

The weather was pleasant, seventy degrees in the late afternoon. Later, a chill would come over the town as the temperature dropped to fifty degrees later that evening. The smell of grilled meat wafted out from the inside grill.

In Deadwood, motorcycle club colors follow rules that are rarely written down but widely understood. Full MC colors, top and bottom rockers, center patches, territory tabs, or 1% diamonds are reserved for legitimate club members, and wearing anything that mimics them without earning the right is considered disrespectful and risky.

Some bars may set their own policies, sometimes allowing colors and sometimes asking for vests to be removed, and those rules are expected to be followed without argument. Whether official or unofficial, the standard is simple. If you're not patched, don't dress like you are, don't touch another rider's colors, and show respect, because in Deadwood, respect is the real rule that's enforced. Johnny knew the rules. He liked to be seen, not scrutinized.

Ringo rolled a silver dollar across his knuckles as he thought. It wasn't real silver, but a cheap replica, dulled just enough to pass at a glance. He let it fall into his palm and closed his fingers around it. With his other hand, he took a sip of his beer.

Johnny was thinking about how he was going to get Johnny Reb into circulation without it coming back to him. Then someone caught his attention.

Off to his right, standing on the sidewalk at the edge of Mustang Sally's patio next to Madame Peacock's clothing store, there was a young man who kept patting down his jacket and pockets. He appeared to be looking for something. He was in his late twenties, wearing a faded open denim jacket. Under it was a black Deadwood tourist T-shirt. His faded jeans were covering what looked like worn boots.

He had a round, boyish face, and his brown, medium-length hair was long enough to fall forward when he moved, but short enough that it never looked styled.

Johnny couldn't see the color of the man's eyes. He did notice that his nose was straight and unremarkable in the way most real noses are, neither sharp nor broad, just slightly weathered at the bridge as if it'd taken its share of wind and sun. Johnny did notice the man's cheekbones stood out more than they should, not gaunt, just sharpened, as if stress had filed him down. The man's jaw was firm, but it looked clenched. Johnny's thoughts became clearer as he watched the man.

The man shrugged to himself and hooked his thumbs in his jacket pockets. He looked around the street. He looked at Johnny.

Johnny waved the man over. The man looked around to make sure Johnny wasn't gesturing to someone else. The men's eyes made contact, and Johnny nodded. The man shrugged and walked over to him.

Johnny took his boots off the fence and leaned forward. "You look like you need something."

"Yeah, I do. You guys got a rolling paper?"

"Kinda bold, aren't you?" Johnny asked.

Johnny's two men laughed.

The young man's face suddenly turned red. "I um, it's not what you think."

Johnny laughed. "What's your name?"

"Mark. Mark Bartholomew."

"Well, Mark, what are you looking for?" Johnny asked.

"I roll my own cigarettes, and I'm out of rolling papers," Mark said.

"Oh, you're not looking for something to put in it?" Johnny asked.

Mark stood up straight. "I don't use. I'm one year sober."

Johnny held up his hands. "Congratulations, amigo. I don't use myself."

Ringo held up his right hand and, without turning around, said, "Jimmy, give me your papers."

Without hesitation, Jimmy pulled out his pack of rolling papers and gave them to Ringo.

Ringo's eyes stayed locked on Mark's eyes as he handed the pack to him.

"Sorry I bothered you," Mark said, finally breaking eye contact.

"Hold up. I've got something else that you might use," Johnny said.

Mark turned back.

Johnny reached into his vest pocket, pulled out a folded, old-looking, gray-green sheet of paper, and handed it to Mark. He turned it over in his fingers and then opened it up to look at it.

"Confederate replica," Ringo said. "Collector junk. Worth more as a story than money."

Mark hesitated, just a beat. "I can't take this, man."

"Paper is paper. Keep it for an emergency or a special occasion," Johnny said.

Mark held up the Confederate bill and the rolling paper before putting it in his jacket pocket. "Thanks. I've got to get to my campsite in the Badlands before sundown. I'll use it later," Mark said.

Johnny nodded. "Yeah, it is getting late. If you leave now, you should make it."

He watched as Mark turned down Wall Street toward the U.S. 14A. Johnny thought Mark must have parked his bike in the same three-story public parking garage they had used. It was just behind Mustang Sally's.

Once Mark was out of sight, Ringo pulled the silver dollar out of his pocket, flicked the coin into the air, and caught it.

"Recovering's just another word for 'not today.'"

Cal shifted uneasily. "You saying…"

"I'm saying," Ringo cut in softly, "that if Johnny Reb can't wake up a ghost, it ain't worth a damn."

The coin disappeared back into Ringo's pocket. He stood, slow and deliberate, his eyes checking to see who was watching him. Out of the corner of his eye, he saw a few women with their men give him a furtive glance.

Johnny smiled to himself at the thought that he had caught their eye, if only for a moment. Something inside him made him feel like he had won something, if only for a moment.

"Let's see," Ringo murmured, almost to himself.

His men stood up and followed Ringo out to the sidewalk.

The low rumble of a motorcycle coming down Wall Street echoed off the buildings. The trio turned and saw Mark on a used Honda Rebel 300. Mark sat low on the bike. Wearing a black half helmet and goggles, boots planted, as he waited for traffic to clear. The bike idled with a steady, muted thrum, compact and unassuming beneath him. Strapped to the back of Mark's bike was a small, light-green, two-man tent, rolled tight in a faded nylon bundle and cinched down with bungee cords. Two folding camp stools were lashed flat on top.

The blue-faded tank bore a few scuffs dulled by time, and the blacked-out engine carried the faint discoloration of heat and miles. His weight had creased the seat where it dipped toward the bars, and the grips shone slightly from use. It wasn't a flashy machine, just a worn, dependable bike. It could still hold at the corners. Then, ready to go at the moment the road opened.

"Frik'in beginner," Jimmy said.

"Yeah, that's a cruiser bike for beginners," Cal chimed in.

"Looks pretty used," Jimmy replied.

Johnny held up his hands in protest. "Eques tiro est. We all had to start riding something."

Jimmy and Cal nodded in agreement as they watched Mark turn and head east on Main Street and disappear in traffic.

Mark followed U.S. 14A as he rode out of Deadwood with the sun slipping toward the horizon, the light thinning and going coppery at the edges. He passed a triangular roadside sign, a plain one with the blunt words THINK and WHY DIE on the other side.

They were installed by the South Dakota Department of Transportation. The state formally documents the program under *"Memorials on State Highways – THINK Signs."* The signs are installed at locations where traffic fatalities have occurred. A single sign represents each fatality. Mark noted there were more than just a few on his way into Deadwood.

Mark had asked his tour guide, Melissa, about them while on a tour of the Broken Boot Gold Mine. She had said that, unfortunately, a lot of those signs were for locals who had lived in the area most of their lives.

How sad, he thought, *I guess complacency kills.*

He also had to admit it made him pay a little more attention to the road. This was something that didn't ask for permission. It made a statement. He stayed on 14A, the road bent easily through Sturgis, then rolled east onto I-90, settling into the long, steady pull toward Rapid City.

Traffic thickened and thinned again, lights flicked on as daylight drained out of the sky. He let Rapid City slide past without stopping, the bike humming, his hands loose but sure on the grips. As he neared the town of Wall, he smiled to himself as he thought about visiting Wall Drug the next morning and getting a cheap cup of coffee, free water, and watching tourists blink awake under fluorescent lights. That was tomorrow's plan.

Mark left the interstate and turned south on 240, the road that would take him into the park. The road dropped gently as the land began to split and fell away. The Badlands opened up slowly and quietly, cracked earth and shadowed cuts stretching out under a darkening sky. He passed through the Pinnacles entrance without ceremony, the park already cooling, already emptying itself of noise.

As Mark rode through the park, the rock formations showed themselves in layers, stacked and exposed like old wounds. The road curved as bands of chalky white, ash gray, rust red, and sun-faded yellow ran through the cliffs and buttes, each color marking a different age. Some layers looked soft and powdery, others sharp and brittle, as if they might shear off at a touch.

Mark's eyes adjusted to the failing light, the colors deepened and bled into one another, and shadows settled into the seams. It was a landscape built from time and pressure, stripped bare and left honest, with nothing to hide and nowhere to pretend it hadn't been broken. He felt small as the bike carried him deeper, toward Sage Creek, where he had chosen as a campsite for the night.

One year sober. He rolled the thought around in his head as the last light bled out of the horizon. A year of staying upright, of choosing exits that led somewhere clean. Jerry would be here soon with a small metal coin that meant something deep. Not just a token. It represented his work and desire to be sober. The engine stayed smooth, the road stayed true. Mark rode on. He felt it would be one of the best days of his life.

Mark made his way to the campsite near Sage Creek and parked his bike. He took his helmet off, set it on the seat, and ran his fingers through his hair. His phone buzzed, and he pulled it out and looked at it. There was a text message from Jerry.

"I am in Rapid Valley. Should be there in an hour."

Mark replied with a thumbs-up emoji and put the phone back in his pocket. The sun was slowly sinking on the horizon. He felt the rolling papers and the Confederate bill. Then a thought struck him.

I'm going to have a cigarette and watch the sunset.

He unlashed one of the stools, carried it a short distance, and sat down on the stool.

Mark reached in and pulled out the Confederate bill and nodded. "Yes, this is a special occasion."

Mark rolled the cigarette slowly and carefully, the way he did most things now. He poured a thin line of tobacco into the paper, breaking it up with his fingertips, spreading it evenly so there were no heavy spots. His hands moved by habit, steady and practiced, thumbs rocking the paper back and forth until the tobacco settled and took shape. He tucked the edge, rolled it closed, and sealed it with a quick pass of his tongue. It wasn't pretty, a little uneven at the ends, but it was tight, and it would burn. He held it for a moment, looking at it as if it mattered, then brought it up to his lips to light it.

Mark cupped the match in his hands, turning his body slightly to block the wind. The flame flared, brief and bright, painting his fingers orange before settling down. He leaned in and touched the tip of the cigarette to the fire, rolling it slowly between his fingers until the paper caught and the tobacco began to glow. He drew once, gently, then again, watching the ember bloom and steady. The smoke came up warm and sharp, and he let it out into the dark, the match dying between his fingers as the night closed back in.

CHAPTER 10

Jerry rode east out of Rapid Valley on U.S. Route 44. The road pulled him straight toward the dark. Behind him, the sun had slid down behind the Black Hills, setting the sky on fire for a few last minutes, deep reds, bruised purples, a thin line of gold clinging to the horizon before it gave up. The light drained fast after that, like someone had turned a dial.

The bike settled into a rhythm. He heard the engine more clearly once the day's din had faded. Jerry felt every vibration through the bars and pegs. The air cooled as he rode, carrying the dry smell of grass and dust, with sage creeping in now and then when the wind shifted. Bugs snapped against his jacket and helmet, little reminders that he wasn't alone out there, even when it felt like it.

By the time he reached the park, night had fully taken over. Entering Badlands National Park after dark felt like riding off the edge of the map. The land flattened and then quietly fell away, invisible beyond the reach of his headlight. The beam carved out a narrow tunnel of road, everything else swallowed by shadow. His senses sharpened. His eyes scanned for movement, ears tuned to changes in the engine's song, hands light but ready on the handlebars.

Above it all, the sky exploded. Without city lights, the stars came hard and bright, scattered thick across the black like spilled salt. The land below was nothing but silhouette and absence, while the sky felt crowded and alive. Jerry rode slower now, respectful of the dark, the contrast pressing in on him. The earth was now unseen and dangerous, the heavens wide open and calm. Somewhere ahead was Sage Creek, a fire, a friend. He kept the bike steady and let the night have its say.

Jerry turned left onto Sage Creek Road, the pavement narrowing as the dark pressed in. He rode a short distance, then pulled over and killed the engine. The sudden quiet felt heavy. He checked the map on his phone, the screen glowed pale against his hands, the blue dot steady and right where it should be.

Overhead, the stars were sharp and countless, filling the sky without competition.

The night made its own small noises. Insects chirped and buzzed in uneven bursts, their sound carrying farther than it should. The air smelled dry and faintly of sage, and it felt cool against his skin. After a minute, he slipped the phone away, restarted the bike, and eased back onto the road.

Ten minutes later, he rolled into Sage Creek Campground. The campground lay quiet and mostly dark, the shapes of grass and earth barely visible beyond his headlight. He slowed, scanning for the familiar outline of a bike, a fire, or any sign that Mark was already there. The engine idled low as Jerry rode in, the stars watching from above and the land keeping its secrets close.

Jerry finally found Mark's bike, pulled up next to it, and killed the engine. He took his helmet off and sat on his bike, getting his bearings. The only sound was the ticking of his bike as it cooled down. There weren't any tents that he could see. Jerry thought that was a little strange for mid-July. He thought maybe he had the wrong place.

No, that couldn't be, that's Mark's bike, Jerry thought.

The other thing that seemed strange was the absence of Mark. Surely, he would have heard the bike coming down the road and seen the headlight, Jerry thought as he got off his bike. He went to one of his saddlebags and pulled out a small flashlight he kept for roadside emergencies at night.

He turned it on and looked at Mark's bike.

That's strange,-the tent and one of the stools are still on the bike. What the hell is going on?

Jerry stopped and listened for a moment. It was quiet except for silence being broken by insects ticking away in the distance. He scanned the area with the flashlight. Wide at first and then lower, letting it skim the ground. That's when he saw them. Footprints. Clear enough in the dirt and dust, leading away from the parked motorcycle and out into the dark. Jerry stood there a moment, then started to walk and followed the tracks with the beam.

Jerry saw him from behind, caught in the narrow cone of the flashlight, and knew something was wrong before his mind could name it. Mark sat on one of the camp stools, shoulders slumped, head bowed forward as if he'd leaned in to listen and never straightened back up. The beam traced the line of his back, the stillness too complete to be sleep.

The moon had risen and hung high and bright, a waxing gibbous washing the campsite in pale light beyond the flashlight's reach, pushing the stars back just enough to make the shadows deeper.

"Mark!" Jerry called out as he approached.

No response.

Jerry called again. "Mark, buddy!"

Jerry stepped closer to Mark. He reached out and touched him. Mark didn't move. Jerry's touch was just enough to make his friend's body slump forward off the stool to the ground like a rag doll. Mark's right shoulder hit the ground first, and the rest of his weight rolled him onto his back. Mark's right arm was pinned under his body at the elbow, and his right hand's fingers were bent slightly. The left arm lay at an awkward angle, without muscle tone. His legs were still bent and leaning to his right. Mark's face wore a serene look. The only thing that stood out was the half-closed eyelids of a dead man.

Jerry noticed the flashlight's light was shaking. He realized he was still holding it. His mind was racing. He had to calm down. Jerry concentrated on his breathing after a few deep breaths, and the shaking subsided.

He reached down and checked for a pulse, hoping, but knowing he would find none. Mark was dead. There was still warmth in Mark's body. Not living warmth but not gone either, heat lingering in Mark's body, it had held by the day and the short time since it had ended.

Jerry's first reaction was to push it down. He needed to think clearly if he was going to find out how his friend had died. It was like a switch had been flipped in his brain, turning off the emotional side and turning on the analytical side.

Jerry checked Mark's fingers. They were cool and stiff, with the remains of a hand-rolled cigarette. The paper had collapsed and burned halfway. He bent closer and smelled Mark's fingers. Only the sour, bitter, acrid bite of nicotine remained. Jerry breathed a sigh of relief. Mark wasn't smoking a joint when he died. If he had, the smell of marijuana would still be on his fingers. It was an old cop technique Jerry had learned the hard way. The only way to get either scent on your fingers was to be in direct contact with the substance.

The next thing Jerry did was examine the paper between Mark's fingers. He put it to his nose. There was no smell of marijuana on it. He put the flashlight in his mouth and poured the remaining contents of the paper into his hand. It looked and smelled like tobacco. He then unrolled the paper. It looked like money, but not like anything he recognized.

Then he thought about it for a moment. *It looks like a Confederate replica.*

Where had he seen one before? Why use it as a rolling paper? Jerry thought.

He shone the flashlight around, and something on the ground near Mark's left side caught the light. He reached over and picked it up. Actually, there were two things. One was a gold-colored casino token, the other a blue one, both from the Wild Bill Bar in Deadwood.

Jerry thought they must have fallen out of Mark's pocket when he slumped over.

"Sorry, buddy, but I have to do this," Jerry said to Mark's lifeless body.

Jerry carefully searched Mark's pockets. Jerry was surprised to find a pack of rolling papers in his friend's pocket. The only other items were a piece of black rock, a pack of matches, a half-full tobacco pouch, and a wallet with a driver's license containing five hundred dollars in cash.

Jerry pocketed the two tokens, the half-burned bill, and the black piece of rock.

He stood up and searched the area again with his flashlight. Satisfied, he pulled out his phone. There was a message telling him he had no service.

"Shit." He shook his head and started to walk back to where his bike was parked. It gave him a moment to think. Something else was coming over him. A feeling he worked every day to keep locked away in a cage. He knew the feeling well, the feeling of his addiction knocking at his psyche. But it wasn't clear if it was his addiction or something else. Was it sorrow, anger, confusion, or a combination of all of them? He had no desire to start using again, but he did have a desire for something. He needed something to fill the void. Jerry pushed those thoughts out of his mind as he reached his bike.

He pulled out his phone again, and this time he had service. Jerry punched in a number and waited.

After a few rings, a young female voice answered. "Bill's Custom Cabinets."

"Hi, do you have anything that keeps the cabinet doors closed?" Jerry asked.

"I'm sorry, we don't. I can have one of our technicians call you shortly," the voice said.

"Sorry to have bothered you," Jerry said and hung up.

Jerry knew the communications protocol. There was no discussion of missions or other sensitive matters over a potentially open network. Further, the conversation was to alert PROACTIVE that he needed to speak to someone over a secure net. Thus, the technician's callback response. The next call Jerry would receive would be over a secure network.

Five minutes later, Jerry's phone buzzed. The caller ID read Bill's Custom Cabinets. As soon as Jerry answered, the call would work like a frequency-hopping radio, never staying on one channel. Instead, it would rapidly jump between many frequencies in a pattern known only to the sender and receiver.

Each burst of the message would be transmitted on a different frequency for a fraction of a second, then the signal would hop again, sometimes hundreds of times per second. To an outsider, it would sound like random noise that's impossible to follow, jam, or intercept. But to the paired phones, synchronized by the exact timing and code, the scattered pieces would snap back together into a clear, continuous conversation. This is similar to the technology that the United States military uses in its communication systems.

Jerry answered, "Hello."

"What's the problem, Amigo?" Greg asked.

Jerry looked around, then crunched near his motorcycle. He spoke in a low tone as he told Greg about what he had found. He did leave out the tokens, the burnt bill, and the black rock. He would tell him later, after he had done some checking on his own.

"Got it. Find a safe place for the night. We will handle it from here," Greg said.

"Understood," Jerry said.

"One last question. Are you all right?" Greg asked.

There was a pause. For a moment, Greg thought the line was dead.

"Yeah, I'll be okay. Just kind of a shock to the system," Jerry said.

Greg thought Jerry's response sounded a little detached, but he wasn't sure.

"Contact me again tomorrow, same time," Greg said.

Jerry looked at the time on his phone. It was 11 p.m. "Acknowledged."

The line went dead. Jerry put on his helmet, started his motorcycle, and made the slow journey out of the Badlands. He knew exactly where he was going to go. Deadwood.

As Jerry turned back onto U.S. 44 and headed west, a phone rang in the Ranger station at Ben Reifel Visitor Center. An anonymous tip was called in about a possible hiker death at Sage Creek campground. This caused a bit of excitement, not because of a potential death, but because they are so rare. Between 2007 and 2024, only six deaths were recorded in the park. It would take a team at least an hour to reach the campground. Everyone knew this was going to be a long night.

As the search party made it to the campground to look for Mark's body, Jerry turned off I-90 toward Deadwood. The speed limit was sixty-five miles per hour on open, straighter stretches outside of town limits. The road was narrow and wooded, with many twists and turns. He slowed to a little under fifty-five miles an hour. There was also wildlife, animals that didn't respect road signs and crossed wherever they felt like it. The last thing he wanted was to become another roadside marker. U.S. 14A stretched ahead in a clean, dark line.

The bike's headlight only shone out about three hundred feet. Jerry did the math in his head. If he had to stop suddenly, it would take him at least 190 feet under good conditions.

The Black Hills rose around him in layers of shadow, pine, rock, and open sky, the stars looked down as silent witnesses to Jerry's journey.

The headlight lit up the THINK triangle signs that lined the roadside. Think. Think. Think. He did think. If he'd taken the risk instead of stopping in Kit Carson? He rehearsed the version of him arriving in time, when Mark is alive and annoyed, when Jerry tells him not to light that cigarette, and Mark actually listens.

If I had only left Texas earlier. I should have told him to meet me at Mount Rushmore, Jerry thought.

The Black Hills closed in and opened again as the highway twisted. Cold air slipped through his jacket and pressed against his chest. He smelled pine and dust and old rain baked back out of the ground.

Jerry's jaw clenched as anger rose in him. Something had killed Mark, and he had a strong suspicion it had something to do with the paper and chips he had found. The only way to find out was to go to Deadwood.

He would get answers. Jerry didn't care how uncomfortable that made people. If words don't work, something else would. Jerry thought about the saying that violence was not the way. He knew in reality that sometimes it was an effective way. The thought didn't scare him. In a way, it brought a smile to his face.

The cravings for addiction come anyway, quiet and patient. Grief and anger have always been their favorite openings. He imagined the relief, the brief shutting-off of pain, and hated how tempting it sounded. His hands tightened on the grips. He matched his breathing to the engine, kept his eyes forward, and kept moving. One more mile. One more choice. Don't stop.

Jerry rounded a corner, and Deadwood's lights finally glowed ahead, a low amber smear against the dark hills. Jerry leaned into the road. He carried guilt, hunger, and a rising anger. He would find answers and wasn't particularly concerned with how he got them.

Jerry slowed as he rolled into Deadwood a little after midnight. The town announced itself with neon before it ever showed him people. The low growl of the motor echoed off the now closed visitor center as he drove slowly by. Another thing Jerry noticed was the temperature change, not cold but noticeably cooler. Enough to make Jerry zip up his jacket. Maybe it was being down in a valley, but for days in the high seventies and mid-eighties, the change was noticeable. It made Jerry wonder if the cold hand of death had followed him.

This is where the road split. Right would take him down Main Street, the left would continue as U.S. 14A, also known as Pioneer Way. He guided the bike slightly right as the road split in front of him. He cruised under the sign that announced in white letters HISTORIC MAIN STREET and underneath it Deadwood, S.D.

Main Street glowed in uneven colors, reds and blues bleeding across the pavement. Traffic was almost non-existent. Jerry felt like a lone cowboy coming into town on his horse in the Old West. The only difference was the names of the buildings, and he was on a motorcycle. If it had been the Old West, he would be in a part of Deadwood called Chinatown.

Chinese immigrants ran laundries, restaurants, and small shops here, which provided essential services to the rough town that depended on them but rarely accepted them.

Jerry had read the history of Deadwood and several other Western myths and legends while being incarcerated. He was familiar with the town's history. He knew that in 1874, Lieutenant Colonel George Custer led a U.S. Army expedition into the Black Hills and publicly confirmed the presence of gold. That announcement sparked the Black Hills Gold Rush. Prospectors poured into the area almost immediately, ignoring treaties that protected the land, and Deadwood sprang up as one of the most significant boomtowns to serve the rush. Then, in 1876, the Federal government demanded that the Lakota and Northern Cheyenne tribes leave their traditional lands and report to reservations, because gold had been found in the Black Hills. Many refused. Custer and the 7th Cavalry were sent to locate and compel these groups to comply. It didn't work out as planned for Custer.

Jerry thought that it was interesting that Custer and Wild Bill Hickok were killed only 39 days apart in 1876, and both were connected to Deadwood. It gave a whole new perspective on cause and effect, Jerry thought. If gold had never been found, then maybe both men would have lived to old age.

Now, I'm in Deadwood. Maybe there is something that draws people to this place more than gold? Jerry thought.

He kept riding farther up the street, past Mr. Wu's and Dahl's Chainsaw Art. The engine echoed off the brick walls of the new hotel buildings on his left. A few people were out, but no one paid the lone rider any attention. Jerry was just another soul who drifted into town and would eventually drift out.

He passed the Mineral Palace Hotel and Gaming on his left and the Brothel on his right. Jerry thought it ironic that the Mineral Palace Hotel and Gaming was open and the Brothel was closed. The Brothel was open continuously from 1876 to 1980. Both took your money, but one made you feel better afterwards.

The buildings were close together, pressed shoulder to shoulder, as if the town had learned long ago how to huddle against the cold and never stopped. Jerry continued up the street and past the Wild Bill Bar that proclaimed on its sign out front that it was the original location of Saloon No. 10, the presumed location of where Wild Bill Hickok drew his last breath. The bar was still open, and through the windows, Jerry saw a few patrons enjoying their drinks.

Farther up on the right, he passed Mustang Sally's, its lights still on, laughter spilling out every time the door opened. Cigarette smoke drifted into the street, stale and sweet, mixed with beer and cooked meat. Life was going on without hesitation. Hunger came over Jerry. He realized he hadn't eaten since noon.

Up on the left, he passed Saloon No. 10, loud even at this hour. He stared into the windows, looking for something.

Mark had been there. What was he doing there? Jerry thought.

Finally, he turned left onto Deadwood Street, away from the noise. The soundscape thinned fast. Music fell behind him, replaced by the steady rumble of his engine and the whisper of tires on pavement. Pine crept back into the smell of things, mixed with damp stone and the faint tang of exhaust. His shoulders stayed tight, his jaw clenched, like his body hadn't yet accepted that the ride was over.

The Historic Iron Horse Inn was on the corner of Deadwood Street and Pioneer Way, across the street from the Adams Museum. Its sign was subdued compared to Main Street's glare. Jerry pulled in. He parked carefully and killed the engine. The sudden silence rang in his ears. He sat there for a moment, helmet still on, listening to the tick of hot metal cooling and the distant echo of laughter drifting up the hill.

When he swung off the bike, the weight of the night settled on him all at once, guilt pressing in his chest, anger humming just under his skin, the ache of wanting something he knew better than to touch. Control still mattered, and he stood there breathing in the cool air until the urge passed enough to move. He looked up at the hills toward Mount Moriah Cemetery. Jerry remembered Wild Bill Hickok was buried up there, and next to him was Calamity Jane.

Deadwood slept around him in fragments, lights on, lights off. The noise faded. He checked in and went to his room. His legs felt heavy as he walked to his room on the second floor. Finally, he made it to his room and closed the door.

Jerry put the helmet on a dresser and stripped off his jacket. His legs felt weak, refusing to hold him up any longer. He dropped to his knees. It started with a sniffle, then his eyes teared up, and the dam broke. A wave of grief swept over Jerry as he sobbed uncontrollably on the floor. Like high tide, waves of grief came crashing in over and over. Guilt, regret, anger, and sorrow mixed into one giant ball. His body shook with grief, then with rage. The feelings would subside for a moment and then well up again. He lay on the floor, crying and growling, sometimes convulsing. He crawled over to a small waste paper basic and heaved what bile was in his stomach. This continued with a series of dry heaves and aftershocks. Jerry's body and brain had had enough and agreed to sleep. There was only so much each could take. Jerry slept on the floor that night. His brain was too tired to dream, and his body was too tired to move.

When Jerry woke up, the sun was coming over the Black Hills. He slowly opened his eyes and blinked at the ceiling of his room. He had a slight headache and was ravenous. Jerry sat up and leaned his back against the foot of the bed. If he didn't know better, he felt like he had a hangover. For a moment, he looked around the room in a panic, making sure he hadn't done anything that broke his sobriety. Jerry sighed in relief that he didn't find any empty bottles or marijuana remains.

Then he caught a sharp, sour reek mingling with the body odor, and he remembered the contribution to the basket. He sniffed himself and caught the body odor. He steadied himself as he stood up, walked to the bathroom, and looked in the mirror.

"You look like you've been shot and missed and shit at and hit," Jerry said to his reflection.

The reflection looked like a man who'd just come off a bender. His hair was a mess, and his face smeared with dirt. His unkempt beard completed the picture. Jerry splashed water on his face. The water felt cold and invigorating. He wiped his face with a towel, then splashed water on his hair and smoothed it with his hand.

He left the bathroom and went down to his bike to get a change of clothes. The air outside was cold. Jerry regretted not picking up his jacket. He went to his bike as fast as he could, grabbed a change of clothes and his hygiene kit, and headed out.

Once back in his room, he showered. The warmth of the shower made Jerry want to stay in longer, but he was hungry and burning daylight. He wanted answers more than comfort. He toweled off, changed, and headed down to the front desk to find someplace to eat. Coincidentally, he was recommended to the Mineral Palace, which opened at 7 a.m. Most places weren't open until 9 a.m. Another benefit was that the food was excellent.

There was no use in taking his bike. The clerk said the place was only a five-minute walk. Jerry left the hotel. The air was cool, much cooler than mid-July should have been. It carried the clean, sharp scent of wet earth and damp asphalt. Low clouds pressed down on the town, dulling the light and flattening the colors. He zipped up his jacket and made his way to Main Street. A fine drizzle began to fall, not enough to soak him, just enough to bead on his jacket and darken the sidewalks.

The street was quiet at that hour. A few cars rolled slowly, tires hissing on the wet pavement. Somewhere, a door opened and closed, followed by the faint clatter of dishes and the muted voices of people already at work. Water dripped steadily from awnings and roof edges, tapping out a soft, irregular rhythm.

A trace of coffee drifted out from somewhere. Jerry's hunger returned. A big breakfast and a strong cup of coffee sounded like heaven at this moment. His stomach growled in response to his thoughts.

Jerry felt the chill settle into his hands and neck, the kind that crept in. He pulled his jacket tighter and kept walking. Boots sounded hollow against the sidewalk, and the drizzle blurred the edges of the town as it woke under a gray sky.

As he passed Saloon No. 10, Jerry's head turned involuntarily as he passed by. The lights were still off inside. He noticed that the place opened at 9 a.m. His fingers felt the casino chips in his pocket.

Finally, Jerry made it to the Mineral Palace and went inside. It felt good to be out of the rain. An overhead crystal chandelier brightly lit the foyer. He went to the front desk and asked for the restaurant. The woman behind the counter was pleasant and told Jerry it was upstairs. She gave him the elevator's directions.

Jerry took the elevator upstairs to the restaurant. The restaurant was almost empty except for a table near a window in the far corner. An older couple sat close together, and the dreary morning light spilled across their table. They spoke quietly, heads bent toward one another, sharing smiles between sips of coffee.

This man appeared to be in his late 50s, with a sturdy, broad build. His broad facial features and slightly weathered complexion suggested experience and an active life. The man sat defensively, his back to the wall, in a position to watch every entrance and exit. Jerry thought the man was either a retired cop or a soldier.

Jerry noticed the man had a relaxed expression and subtle smile that conveyed quiet confidence. He had short, neatly trimmed gray hair, a matching gray mustache and goatee, and wore wire-rim glasses that added to his thoughtful, practical look. He had a no-nonsense style. Dressed in a navy-blue collared shirt, blue jeans, and black boots.

He could only see the woman from the side. She appeared to be of similar age, with a fuller, solid build. Her blond hair, slowly turning gray, was pulled back, and wearing glasses. She was shorter than the man and wore a bright blue top, blue jeans, and white tennis shoes. Her light gray puffy jacket hung over the back of her chair.

Jerry noticed how easy they were together, how unhurried. It made him wonder whether, someday, he might return to a place like this with someone of his own, sharing a quiet breakfast. But that day was not today. He turned his attention back to the room and found a seat on the opposite side of the room from the couple. He also made sure he had his back to the wall. He too sat by a window overlooking Main Street.

He ordered black coffee, three eggs, bacon, and biscuits for breakfast. When it came, he focused on nothing else. Jerry was so engrossed in his breakfast that he didn't notice the couple had left. Once breakfast was finished, he looked at the clock on the wall. It was 8:30 a.m. There were at least another thirty minutes for him to wait. Jerry ordered another cup of coffee and looked out at Main Street.

He noticed plants hanging from the streetlamps lining the street, having missed them on his way in. What caught his attention was a small white truck stopping at each one, and a person getting out to water them, even though it was drizzling. That made no sense.

Then he caught himself. AA had taught him that understanding wasn't the entry fee. Action came first. The man in the truck didn't stop to argue with the weather or second-guess the plan; he just followed the route, light after light, doing what he was told. The plants didn't care where the water came from, either. They took what reached them and held on.

Jerry let the thought settle. His best thinking had always insisted on clarity before movement, and it had nearly killed him. What had kept him sober wasn't insight or certainty, but showing up, meetings, calls, small, repetitive actions that sometimes felt redundant, especially on the good days. Jerry didn't have to understand why it worked. He just had to keep stopping, keep watering, even when it was already raining.

He took a sip of his coffee and looked at the clock. It was ten minutes to nine. Jerry pushed the idea of the plants out of his head. Mark was dead, and he needed to find out why. He took one more drink of his coffee and got up. He threw some money down on the table.

I'll start at Saloon No. 10, Jerry thought.

There was enough to pay the bill and tip the waitress. He pulled his jacket on and left the restaurant.

Out on the street, traffic was picking up, and shops were opening. It had stopped drizzling, but the overcast sky still hid the sun. Jerry zipped up his jacket against the cold. He leaned into the chill as he headed to the saloon. Jerry heard the rumble of motorcycles coming down the street toward him. He looked up and saw three bikers.

Johnny Ringo and his two henchmen were riding down the street. Johnny drove a black-and-chrome Harley-Davidson Fat Boy; the other two were black-and-chrome cruisers. All three riders wore leather jackets, jeans, and boots. Johnny wore a cowboy hat. His two men wore black skull caps. Once they passed Mustang Sally's, the three turned left on Wall Street to the parking garage. Their engines echoed off the walls. The sound seemed louder as it broke the morning quiet.

Jerry made it to Saloon No. 10. The building had a dark wooden façade with horizontal boards and a centered doorway marked by the saloon's name. Two red benches sat out front beneath old, dark red wagon wheels that covered the round windows on either side of the doorway.

Jerry opened the door and walked inside. The place had a rustic look. There weren't any patrons in the bar at this time of day, but it would fill up soon enough. Jerry liked that. It meant he had fewer people to deal with. The place was lit by electrified 1800s replicas of oil lamps, with brass bases and clear glass chimneys. Their lights cast a yellowish glow, giving the place an old-time atmosphere. As he looked around, he saw a long polished wooden bar lined with modern barstools on the left side of the room. The shelves behind the bar were packed with bottles of different types of alcohol. Also, there were signs and memorabilia hung in almost every available space in the place.

An older man in Old West attire stood behind the bar, preparing it for the day's service. He stopped what he was doing as Jerry approached.

"What'll it be, partner?" the man said.

Jerry fished out the two gambling tokens from his pocket and placed them on the counter.

The man picked up the gold one and looked at it. "This is one of ours."

He set it down and picked up the blue one and smirked. "Sorry, buddy. This isn't a poker chip at all. It comes from a bar across the street, called Wild Bill's Bar. It's a souvenir they sell."

Jerry looked surprised. "Oh. My friend gave them to me. He's got a sense of humor."

"Well, at least you can try the gold one on one of our slots on the other side of the bar," the man said, pointing to another room with slot machines against the wall.

Jerry thought for a moment. He didn't want to look too suspicious, so he left right away. "Sure, I'll try it, why not?"

"Good luck," the man said.

Jerry went into the next room. He slid the token into the slot and heard it drop out of sight with a dull metallic click. The machine hummed to life as he pulled the handle, and the reels blurred into bands of color. For a second, it looked like something might line up. Jerry's heart quickened, then the motion slowed, and the symbols fell out of step, cherry, bell, lemon, each stopping on its own time. The machine gave a flat, final clunk. No lights flashed. No music played. Jerry's lips squirmed with the quiet acknowledgment of a loss as the reels settled and the slot went still again.

He shrugged.

What did you expect? The odds are in favor of the house, Jerry thought.

He turned and started for the door of the bar. He looked up above the door and saw behind a glass-front display a simple wooden chair labeled "Wild Bill's Death Chair." A light inside the case illuminated the chair. The case itself was lined in red velvet, and the chair had a brown Old West-style gun belt with a revolver in the holster hanging from the left side of the chair's back.

The chair itself was a mid-19th-century wooden side chair, sometimes called a ladder-back or slat-back style. It's utilitarian rather than decorative. It was made for everyday use in saloons and homes. It reflected the frontier's practical furniture standard rather than anything ornate or comfortable.

Jerry turned back to the old man. "Is that the real chair?"

"Sure is. If you come back here in about an hour, we do a reenactment of the shooting," the man said.

"Yeah. I think I'll do that." Jerry turned and left the bar.

He crossed the street and saw the old, brown and white neon sign that read, "Wild Bill's Bar" hung perpendicular to a building. The building's façade was a two-story reddish-brown brick structure with lighter stone trim outlining the windows and edges, giving it a solid, late 19th-century look. Two tall, rectangular windows on the second floor reflected the overcast gray sky, their glass clean and modern against the older masonry.

A large horizontal sign stretched across the front just above the ground-floor windows. It read "ORIGINAL LOCATION OF SALOON NO. 10 – HISTORIC SPOT OF THE OLD WEST 1876," painted in bold, maroon lettering on a sandy beige background. Below it, wide windows reflected nearby buildings and the street.

Hanging perpendicular to the sidewalk over the main entrance was a rectangle-shaped gray weathered sign with white letters carved into it that stated that this was the HISTORIC SITE SALOON NUMBER 10 WHERE WILD BILL WAS SHOT ON AUGUST 2, 1876.

This must be the place, Jerry thought as he opened the door.

The place seemed busy compared to the other one. All of the patrons were casually dressed. Probably all of them were tourists, Jerry thought. They stood and sat throughout the room. Some leaned on the bar, others gathered near tables.

The place looked like another long, narrow historic saloon, filled with people and Old West décor. The polished wooden bar ran the length of the room on the left, its surface worn smooth and crowded with menus, glasses, and small displays. Behind the bar rose an ornate dark-wood backbar with carved details, shelves of bottles, and glowing lamps. The one thing that stood out to Jerry was the large front windows that let in natural light, making the place feel larger than the bar he had come from.

The high ceiling was covered in pressed tin panels with decorative patterns, reflecting light from chandeliers, ceiling fans, and recessed fixtures. The wooden floorboards stretched the length of the saloon, their grain and scuffs visible from decades of use.

Mounted deer heads and antlers lined the right-hand wall, spaced between framed photos, clocks, and historic signs. Small round tables and tall stools sat beneath them, some occupied, others pushed close together. The walls were a mix of wood paneling and lighter-painted sections, heavily decorated yet orderly.

Jerry took his time walking around the place. He wasn't going to make the mistake he'd made last time and start asking questions. He wasn't even sure what he was looking for; the two tokens and the burnt paper were all he had, proof only that Mark had been in these bars at some point. They didn't bring him any closer to why he'd died. Still, the longer Jerry stayed, the easier it felt to keep moving, to let the room quiet and sharpen around him in a way he recognized but didn't name.

He walked to the far end of the room, where a wooden stairwell descended, and at the bottom, a set of swinging doors blocked the view beyond. The staircase was narrow and steep, made of dark, polished wood with visible wear along the steps and handrails.

Centered between the two stair rails was a framed historical sign mounted above the two swinging wooden doors. A picture featured Wild Bill Hickok and text explaining that this was the historic site where he was killed in 1876 at Saloon No. 10. An illustrated hand pointed down to the doors.

Okay, so which one is it? Is it here or the bar I just came from? Jerry thought.

"You can go down and look around if you leave a donation," a woman's voice said to his left.

Startled, Jerry turned to the voice. "Hi, how much?"

The woman was standing behind the bar. She looked to be in her late forties and had aged well. She had a pleasant round face and a natural smile. Her chestnut-brown hair was cut to shoulder length. She wore a light blue blouse and had a medium build, suggesting she was athletic. Jerry estimated she was about 5'6".

"Usually ten dollars," the woman said.

Jerry reached into his pocket and pulled a twenty-dollar bill from his money clip.

He handed her the money. "Will this do?"

"Hold on, I'll get you change," she said.

Jerry waved his hand. "Don't worry about it."

"Thanks. Just put the rope back when you head down the stairs," she smiled.

"Yes, ma'am," Jerry said as he turned to head down the stairs.

He lifted the velvet rope off the hook and descended the stairs, after making sure to put the velvet rope back.

He heard other voices as he pushed open the doors to enter the room. Once he passed the doors and they swung closed, he took two more steps and was in the room. Jerry's eyes adjusted to the light.

The room was in the Old West style, with wooden floors and wood-paneled walls. He looked around and saw the man from breakfast. He looked even bigger standing up, his size alone enough to intimidate most people. He wore a black peacoat and a brown leather cowboy hat, casually snapping photos with his phone.

Johnny Ringo, Dale, and Cal were also there, murmuring to each other. They were pointing and looking at some of the other memorabilia.

Jerry saw that two round tables were spaced across the room, each surrounded by mismatched wooden chairs. Playing cards were scattered across the tabletops, and a black hat rested on one. The walls were decorated with mounted antlers, framed photos, signs, and old tools, while some stools were made from tree stumps, their legs unfinished. Some small barrels lined the edges of the room. The space was obviously staged to look like a preserved saloon frozen in time.

On one of the tables closest to where Jerry had entered was a round, scarred wooden table. Simple wooden chairs surrounded the table, each mismatched and slightly angled, reinforcing the sense of an abrupt departure. The tabletop was worn smooth, marked with dark rings and scratches from years of use. Scattered across it were playing cards, some face up, others stacked or half-spread, suggesting a game frozen mid-hand. Near the center sat a black, wide-brimmed felt hat, its crown slightly creased, resting casually as if its owner just stood up.

In front of the hat lay a revolver placed atop a small spill of amber-colored liquid, soaking into cards and paper beneath it. The gun's dark metal contrasted sharply with the pale cards. When Jerry got closer, he could see the cards. They were the infamous dead man's hand of aces and eights. The hand that Wild Bill Hickok was holding when he was shot dead.

A weird hush slid over Jerry, like the room had tilted without moving. This was it. The spot. The postcard murder every drunk history buff knew by heart.

Johnny jabbed a thumb at the floor. "Yup. Right here. Where some chicken-shit coward put one in Wild Bill."

Jerry blinked at him. "What?"

Johnny didn't miss a beat. "This is where some pussy shot Hickok in the back."

"Uh—no," a voice said.

Every head turned.

The man stood off to the side, old, broad, built like gravity still took him seriously.

Johnny scowled. "And you know that how?"

"Because the room's backwards," the man said calmly. "Completely ass-end wrong."

Dale puffed up. "You saying that like it means something."

The old man turned his eyes on Dale. Not angry. Measuring. Dale felt himself shrink and hated it.

"Fair question," the man said, smiling.

Jerry leaned in. "I'm listening."

The man dragged a chair out and sat like a schoolteacher about to ruin a favorite myth. He carefully took off his hat and set it down.

Johnny's jaw locked. *Who the hell is this clown?*

"Deadwood grew fast," the man said. "Tents. Shacks. Burned down. Burned again. Flooded. Rebuilt higher every time." He jerked a thumb over his shoulder. "That's why you walked *down* into this room. Killer came in behind me, not where you're pointing."

Johnny snorted. "So they flipped it. Big deal."

Jerry said, "But it's still the place?"

"Yeah," the man said.

Johnny snapped, "How the hell would you know?"

The man looked right at him and smiled, "You remember where you were when someone close to you died?"

Dale nodded. Cal too. Johnny didn't—but his hands curled anyway.

"People in 1876 remembered," the man went on. "They wrote it down. Mapped it. Marked buildings, street angles. The saloon burned, but the spot didn't change."

Johnny clenched his fists. "That chair's real."

The man went quiet, rubbed his beard, as he decided how to answer.

Johnny sneered. "See? Full of shit."

The man's head snapped up. His eyes sharpened. Then he laughed, deep, ugly, amused. The sound rolled through the room and crushed Johnny's last scrap of confidence.

"You see the chair I'm sitting in?" the man said. "Same style as that 'death chair.' The problem is this style didn't exist until the 1900s." He tapped the seat. "So, unless Bill stuck around twenty-five extra years, that ain't his chair."

He pointed to a squat tree-stump stool nearby. "That one? Yeah. That looks about right. Fancy for its day."

Jerry barked out a laugh. "Now that's funny."

Johnny's face went red. He knew leaving would look weak. He had to say something.

"Why'd he get killed?" Johnny shot back.

"Contract," the man said.

Jerry frowned. "Go on."

"Hickok knew he was slipping, between his health and drinking. He wasn't a lawman anymore. His friend offered him a chance to work in his gold mine. That lasted a day. He went back to what he knew, and that was cards."

The man shrugged. "Some folks didn't want a famous lawman around their town. Some thought he'd cause trouble. Or order."

Jerry nodded. "Makes sense."

"And funny thing," the man added, standing. "Town got a real lawman almost immediately after. Coincidence? Maybe. Maybe not."

He put his hat on and headed for the stairs. The others stepped aside to let the man go by.

Jerry called after him, "That was solid. How'd you learn all that?"

The man paused and looked back.

"Retired military," he said. "I wanted to visit some of the places I defended."

Then he smiled. "Also helps to talk to locals. The bar manager upstairs knows a lot of history. Especially because she grew up in Deadwood."

Then he climbed the steps, leaving Johnny with nothing but red ears and a history lesson he didn't ask for—and couldn't beat.

The old man was halfway up the stairs when Johnny spoke again, softer now, like he didn't want the room turning on him.

"What'd you do in the military?" Johnny asked. "Since you know so damn much."

The man stopped. Didn't turn around.

"Infantry. Close with and kill the enemy," he said.

"Where?" Johnny pushed.

"I would tell you, but I don't think you could find them on a map." The man kept walking.

Johnny snorted, but it came out thin. "That's not an answer."

The man looked back over his shoulder. His eyes passed over Johnny and settled on Jerry instead.

"What's it to ya?"

Johnny didn't have an answer.

The man adjusted his hat and went up the rest of the steps. The door swung closed behind him. The room breathed again.

For a moment, nobody spoke. Jerry stared at the empty stairwell.

The man hadn't argued like a historian. He'd briefed like someone who'd done it thousands of times. He was a braggart and more than a tourist. The man had earned his peace.

Jerry knew the man learned the difference between what people *say* happened and what really happened.

Jerry exhaled slowly.

Johnny shifted beside him, restless, still looking for something to push against.

"There's no point," Jerry said, almost to himself.

Johnny frowned. "What?"

Jerry shook his head. "Nothing."

But it wasn't nothing.

Jerry looked at Johnny and his men.

"The guy seems to know a lot."

"Whatever," Johnny said.

His anger showed as he started up the stairs. His two men followed. Jerry watched them leave. The doors swung closed. Jerry stood looking around with a new perspective on the place.

Once Johnny and his men were outside the bar halfway up the street, Johnny whirled around to face his men.

"Find him and bring him to me," Johnny ordered.

"The Army guy?" Dale asked.

"No, that other pussy. The one who laughed at me," Johnny growled.

"Sure. Johnny, whatever you say," Cal said.

CHAPTER 11

Jerry spent the day trying to clear his head after the history lesson and the personal one he received at the bar. He had ridden without his helmet, which felt liberating. One of the things he wanted to see was Wild Bill Hickok's grave at Mount Moriah Cemetery. He managed to keep his thoughts at bay, but kept going back to Mark's death. The sun had set just as Jerry pulled into the parking lot behind the Historic Iron Horse Inn. He needed to check in with Greg in a few hours.

The lot wasn't very crowded, just few cars and a white delivery van parked near the back. He parked next to the building, killed the engine, flipped the kickstand down, and dismounted his bike. The Fat Boy was still ticking softly as it cooled. The building loomed behind him, brick and dark windows, with a single security light casting a weak yellow cone across the lot. It was quiet in the way only Deadwood could manage, peaceful, but never empty.

Jerry walked to the hotel. He slowed. Not because he saw anything, but because the night stopped behaving normally.

The usual sounds didn't disappear. They just... thinned. No laughter drifting from Main. No passing engine. Even the wind seemed to hold back.

Jerry turned halfway, hand drifting near his jacket pocket. He told himself he was tired. That grief made patterns out of nothing.

He heard something behind him. Once. Then again.

Two sets of footsteps. Measured. Unhurried.

Jerry stopped. "Let me guess," he said, not turning all the way. "This is where I find out I parked in the wrong spot?"

A voice answered from behind him. "Something like that."

Jerry turned. They stood just outside the reach of the security light, two men. He had seen the two earlier at Wild Bill's Bar.

"I know you guys," Jerry said as he slowly adjusted his feet into a martial arts fighting stance.

"Boss wants to talk," Cal said.

Jerry glanced toward the inn.

"I'm done talking tonight," Jerry said. "Try again tomorrow."

Dale stepped closer.

"Johnny Ringo doesn't wait for tomorrow," he said.

Jerry laughed. "You've got to be kidding me. If your boss is Johnny Ringo, then I'm Doc Holiday."

Cal took a step forward. "Time to go, Doc."

Jerry's jaw tightened. "Didn't ask to meet him."

"Deadwood's funny that way," Dale said.

Dale threw a punch that came from the side.

Jerry moved on instinct. His shoulder turned into the blow instead of his face. Pain cracked through him, sharp and bright.

This guy can throw a punch, Jerry thought.

He brought his arms up fast, forearms crossing in front of his face as the blows came in, knuckles thudding into bone instead of teeth. Each hit jolted down to his shoulders, but he stayed tight, chin tucked, eyes squinting through the gaps.

When the rhythm broke, he stepped in.

Jerry dropped one arm just long enough to turn his body and drove his elbow forward, hard and short, into Dale. Bone met flesh with a dull crack. The man's head snapped back, and he staggered.

For half a second, it felt possible.

Then Cal took his legs out.

Jerry hit the ground hard, knocking the wind out of him. Dale was on him instantly, knee on his chest, forearm grinding across his throat.

"Don't make this worse," Dale said quietly. "Like I said. Johnny wants to see you."

Cal pulled a canvas bag over Jerry's head, the smell of old sweat and dust filling his lungs. His hands were yanked behind him, rope biting fast and sure.

Jerry decided not to fight. He thought if they wanted to kill him, they would have done it and left. He needed to conserve his energy and wait for the right opportunity.

He thought of Mark, of all the wrong turns that led here. Of how every excuse he'd made lately sounded thinner now. Jerry knew that Johnny Ringo didn't send men for nothing. Ringo wanted something, or Jerry would be dead.

And whatever Jerry had been circling since Deadwood, it had finally decided to close the distance. Jerry felt himself lifted off the ground and roughly thrown onto a metal floor and heard doors close.

I must be in the delivery van I saw when I pulled in, Jerry thought.

Jerry heard the van doors close. The engine started and settled into a steady hum.

They pulled onto a paved street. A smooth left, then a longer right. Jerry counted turns as he tried to remember the way they were going. The town was in a valley. There couldn't be too many places they could go. When the road began to rise, he braced his boots against the back of the van. Hills narrowed the options. He didn't hear any other traffic, which meant he was probably heading up Lincoln Street. He had driven up it on his way to the cemetery. The angle was almost 15 degrees. He felt the van make a sharp, slow left. Jerry thought they must be pulling into a driveway. There was a small squeak of the brakes as the van stopped.

He heard the back doors open. Hands grabbed him on either side and pulled him out onto his feet.

"If you scream or fight, you're done," a voice said in a low voice.

Jerry thought it was Dale but couldn't be sure.

The same hands pulled, half-dragged him forward. Jerry heard the squeak of a door opening. Then the sound shifted from the hard thud of walking on pavement to the hollow thud of walking on a wooden floor. He heard the door close. Jerry was pushed down onto a chair. The hood was pulled off his head. His eyes took a moment to adjust to the light.

The garage smelled of old oil, pine sap, and dust baked into the wood. It was larger than it needed to be, with a ceiling high enough that the rafters disappeared into shadow. Bare bulbs hung in a straight line, casting hard circles of light and leaving the corners dim.

Jerry could hardly believe what he saw. At the end of the room, Johnny sat in a large chair on a three-tiered dias. A single light hung above him, casting a cone of white light over Johnny and the chair. The light was slightly behind the chair, so Johnny's face was in shadow.

The massive, throne-like armchair was carved from dark wood; it had a heavy presence. The back rose high above the seat, crowned with ornate scrollwork and a carved crest that suggested authority. Deep red leather was tufted across the tall backrest, the buttons pulled tight so the surface puckered inward like old armor worn thin.

The arms were thick and squared, wrapped in the same dark leather and supported by carved figures that resembled lion faces, with claws and curling shapes carved into the wood. The legs were short but solid, each one blocky and reinforced.

The chair wasn't furniture, but more of a declaration. It was meant for sitting still while others stood, watched, and waited.

Johnny rested his elbows on the armrests. His fingers steepled as if he were studying Jerry.

This guy has some serious issues. What did Freud say? "Men are all heroes in their dreams," Jerry thought.

There was a long pause.

"You thought that was funny," Johnny said, his voice echoed slightly

"Which part?" Jerry asked with a smile.

"That old man's story," Johnny responded.

"He corrected a detail," Jerry said. "History survives that kind of thing."

"You don't correct me," Johnny said. "When I talk, people listen. They nod. That's the arrangement."

"Or they don't feel like pushing back."

Johnny's hands clenched.

"You don't tell me what happened," Johnny said. "I tell you.

"I build people," Johnny said. "I decide who's useful and who's forgotten. Respect makes the difference."

Jerry looked to his left and right, trying to find Dale and Cal in the dark.

"You build noise," Jerry said. "Respect has nothing to do with it."

Johnny suddenly stood. Towering over Jerry. Something sharp flickered behind Johnny's eyes, then vanished.

"Careful," Johnny said. "That kind of honesty gets men hurt."

"Only if they need to be liked. You are pretty brave with two of your guys in the room and my hands tied behind my back."

Johnny laughed. "Hardly. But I like you. You're steady. Most people in this town talk too much when they're nervous."

He snapped his fingers. Jerry heard movement behind him and felt the pressure on his wrists release as the bindings were cut away. Before he could turn, a sharp blow struck the side of his head, snapping it sideways and stealing his balance.

"That's a reminder that we are still here," Cal said.

Jerry stood up and rubbed his wrists.

"I didn't hear you," Jerry whispered.

Cal stepped forward. Jerry noticed a pistol in Cal's waistband.

"What did you say?" Cal said, stepping forward.

"I didn't hear you," Jerry whispered again.

Cal stepped as his arm came forward to strike Jerry again. Jerry side-stepped and blocked Cal's arm, locking it in and exposing his midsection. Jerry, in quick fashion, grabbed the man's pistol and wrapped his forearm around Cal's throat and pulled back. Jerry pointed the gun at Johnny.

Johnny slowly clapped his hands. "You are good."

"Yeah, I've heard that before. But, I'm done talking to you."

Dale stood still as he looked at Jerry. He watched as Jerry moved to the door with Cal.

"Dale, shoot Cal," Johnny calmly said.

Cal's face suddenly lit up in surprise. Dale fumbled his gun out of his waistband. He half-pointed at Cal.

"Shoot him," Johnny ordered.

Jerry kept moving toward the door with Cal. Dale's hand shook as he raised it and took aim.

"Stop!" Johnny yelled.

He walked over to Dale and took the gun from his hand. Then, Johnny struck Dale on the head with it.

"Ow!" Dale cried, his hands flying up to his head.

"Wait outside," Johnny snarled.

Johnny pointed the gun at Cal. Jerry suddenly caught the scent of urine and heard it dripping onto the floor.

Johnny put his gun on the ground, then slowly stood and raised his hands.

"Kill him if you want to, I have no use for him," Johnny said.

"Kick the gun over to me," Jerry said.

Johnny kicked the gun at Jerry. "Everything's on your side. I just want to talk."

Jerry moved his foot to step on the gun. He thought about his options. What should he do? What did this guy want? Right now, he had a hostage and two guns. But there were still three of them, and they were on their home turf.

"You can keep the guns. I just want to talk. It would be easier if you let Cal change his clothes. If you don't like what you hear, you can leave, no questions asked," Johnny said in an unusually calm tone.

What is this guy up to? This punk, Cal, is about to crap himself next, and I don't want to kill him for no reason, Jerry thought.

Jerry released his hold on Cal and pushed him forward. Cal was shaking.

"Get out!" Johnny commanded.

Cal ran to the door. He slammed into it as he tried to push it open. His hands fumbled with the door as he pulled it open and ran outside. Then, as an afterthought, he ran back and slammed it closed.

The door slam echoed for a moment.

"That's better," Johnny said.

Jerry held the gun on him as he picked up the other pistol and tucked it in his waistband.

"What do you want to talk about?" Jerry asked.

"What's your name?" Johnny asked.

"Doc Holiday," Jerry shot back.

Jerry watched anger flash across Johnny's face, then a wave of calm returned.

I must have struck a nerve, Jerry thought.

"Okay, Doc, if you prefer. I need someone I can trust to do a job," Johnny said.

"Was this some type of job interview?" Jerry asked.

Jerry watched as Johnny walked back to his seat and casually sat down.

"You can handle yourself. I need men like you," Johnny said.

"Hire better," Jerry said.

"I've bought plenty of men. I have a whole gang of them. Money can't buy you talent," Johnny said.

Jerry waved the gun toward the door. "What about those two?"

"They'll be fine. I always need gofers," Johnny said.

Jerry studied Johnny. He seemed impulsive and erratic, and Jerry would bet Johnny was only capable of shallow emotional attachments, all the signs of a sociopath. After seeing the chair and how he acted in the bar, Jerry knew Johnny was definitely a narcissist.

"What's the job?" Jerry asked.

Johnny waved to the chair where Jerry had first sat. "Please have a seat and let's talk like men."

Jerry took the offered seat, but still kept his gun pointed at Johnny.

"I need you to pick up two things and deliver them to me in Tombstone, Arizona."

Jerry raised an eyebrow as his face couldn't hold his surprise.

"What's in it for me?" Jerry asked.

"What do you want?"

"What do you have to offer?"

Johnny's face lit up in surprise. "I've never had that question asked. You are a fascinating man."

"I do what I can," Jerry said.

"First thing is, you can keep the guns, but please stop pointing them at me," Johnny said.

"No contract hits. No drug running. This would be a one-and-done delivery. Once I'm done, I'm out. I leave with enough money that I won't have to work for a very long time," Jerry said.

"Agreed," Johnny said.

Jerry thought Johnny's response was a bit too quick, as if he had more to hide. Jerry knew the only way he was going to find out was to take the job.

"I have one other request. Keep your lackies away from me. I work for you and you alone. Understood?"

"Understood," Johnny responded.

"I also want to drive myself back to my hotel," Jerry said.

"I don't blame you. Just leave the keys under the seat." Johnny smiled.

"Let's hear what you want me to do?"

"Simple delivery. I charge other gangs a fee to use my routes. The Buckskins are due. I want you to go to Yellowstone Park to get the money. It should be ten thousand dollars. Then go to Moab, pick up some printing plates, give the engraver five thousand, and bring them and the rest of the money to me in Tombstone."

"I'm a bag man? You've got to have someone else who can do this for you?" Jerry asked.

"You yourself said hire better. I'm taking your advice." Johnny smiled again.

Jerry knew he was caught in his own words. He had dug his hole with his own mouth. This guy wasn't stupid. Johnny had set this whole thing up, and Jerry had fallen for the bait. He would play the game a little longer. He really didn't have a choice.

Jerry did some quick math in his head. It would take him about three days to complete the trip. "That's a lot of ground to cover."

"You will need to leave tomorrow morning. The delivery is scheduled for 6 a.m. the following morning. I want you to go across Montana, not across Wyoming. You need to enter the park through the north entrance," Johnny said.

"That's going to take at least nine hours. That's a long ride for one day," Jerry answered.

"That's not my problem. Timing is everything. The man with the money will only be there for ten minutes. Then head out through West Yellowstone and down to Moab," Johnny said.

"Is there a deadline for Moab?"

"No, but I need you to be in Tombstone by Saturday."

Jerry finally put the pistol he'd been holding in his waistband, alongside the other gun he'd seized. "What stops me from taking the money and the printing plates?"

"You're not a stupid man. You don't strike me as a thief. You wouldn't steal ten thousand dollars and some printing plates you can't use. One of my guys might. That's why I'm hiring you," Johnny explained.

This guy is smooth. He knows how to flatter you even when he's at a disadvantage. I wonder how he plays poker. But isn't this what we're doing? Jerry wondered.

Johnny put two fingers in his mouth and made a sharp whistle. The door flew open. Cal and Dale rushed in hard. Jerry turned fast, already moving, both pistols up and steady, barrels tracking them as they crossed the threshold.

Cal checked himself mid-stride, boots skidding as he saw the pistols leveled at his chest. Dale froze a half step behind him, hands spreading without being told, weight shifting back as if he might bolt. Neither spoke. The room went still, all three men measuring each other.

Johnny stood and pointed at Jerry. "Doc Holiday here will be driving himself home."

Cal nodded and fished the keys out of a clean pair of jeans and threw them at Jerry's feet.

"You are not to bother him again. Now leave us," Johnny ordered.

The two men left as fast as they had arrived.

Jerry reached down and picked up the keys.

"I guess I'll be leaving now."

Jerry moved slowly toward the door. He opened it with care, checking to make sure Cal and Dale weren't waiting outside. When he saw no sign of them, he headed for the van. He circled it, then checked inside for any hidden surprises. Finding none, he climbed in, started the engine, and pulled out of the driveway. As he looked around, his suspicion was confirmed. He was on Lincoln Street.

Back in the building, Cal came in a side door and walked up to Johnny. "Would you have really let me get shot?"

Johnny laughed and patted Cal on the back. "No, I still have a use for you."

Dale came into the room. "What's so funny?"

"We were just laughing about Johnny not shooting me," Dale said with a strained smile.

An hour later, Jerry was back in his room. He picked up his phone and dialed a familiar number.

"Bill's Custom Cabinets," a female voice said.

Jerry grinned at the sound of a familiar voice. "Can someone call me about an estimate?"

"It's a little after hours. It may be four hours before I can find someone to call you back," the woman said.

"That would be great, just great. I'll be waiting patiently," Jerry said and hung up.

Jerry knew what she meant. He was two hours late for his check-in. With every missed hour, another layer of assets was spun up to find him, quiet at first, then less so. Before anything escalated, they had to be stood down.

The conversation itself was coded, the kind of verbal tripwire sometimes used in the military to confirm whether someone was compromised. When the woman said it would be four hours, she wasn't talking about time. She was telling Jerry to use the fourth letter of his last name to build a sentence. *Meegler.* If he'd chosen any other letter, a different protocol would have triggered—one that involved a lot more kinetic energy.

A few moments later, the phone rang. He looked at the caller ID and answered the phone.

"Hello."

There was a pause.

The next voice he heard was Greg's. "You missed your check-in. What happened?"

Jerry tried to interpret Greg's tone. He couldn't tell if he was irritated or concerned.

Jerry recounted everything that had happened with Johnny Ringo, from the day's first contact to the last uneasy exchange that night.

There was another pause. "There were two explosions in Arizona last night, about the same time you were in the Badlands. It's suspected that the cartel spilled over from the border."

"Are they related?" Jerry asked.

"Garrett thinks so. He still has friends in the ATF. They call him on the sly when they need help. A drug lab got incinerated. A car bomb followed. Military-grade explosives were used. Just not U.S. military grade explosives."

Jerry raised an eyebrow in surprise. "Interesting."

"Back to Johnny Ringo. Keep digging. We'll rendezvous in Tombstone. If it turns out to be nothing, we stand down. But if it isn't, we need to get ahead of it."

"Understood," Jerry said.

"Keep in touch at each way point you stop at," Greg said.

"What if I don't have cell service?" Jerry asked.

Greg laughed. "The helmet we gave you does more than Bluetooth your phone."

Jerry laughed. "I should have known."

"Try not to lose it," Greg said.

"I won't. Just one more question," Jerry said.

There was a long pause.

"Any word on Mark?" Jerry asked.

"Still waiting on the report. Alex will review it as soon as she can get a copy," Greg said.

"Thanks," Jerry said.

"How are you holding up?" Greg asked.

"I'm working through it," Jerry said.

"You know you're not alone out there," Greg said.

"Yeah, I know. Thanks. I need to get some rest. It's a long ride tomorrow," Jerry said, trying to change the subject.

"Sure, buddy. Out here," Greg said, and the line went dead.

Jerry sat down on his bed and looked at his helmet.

"I should have known."

CHAPTER 12

Jerry rolled out of Deadwood on U.S. 212, just after daylight. The bike felt tight under him. Cold air cut through the jacket, finding every gap it could. The Black Hills kept him busy, curves, elevation, and trees close enough to clip a mirror if you got sloppy.

Then the sky and the road opened up.

Wyoming hit like a switch. The road went straight and stayed that way. Wind shoved at the bike hard enough to make him lean to stay centered. Trucks passed fast and close. The engine noise became constant, something he stopped noticing after the first hour.

His stops for gas were short. Helmet off. Card in. Tank filled. Then back on the bike.

Miles stacked up with nothing to block the sky. Out in the distance were radio towers, with fence lines stretching to the horizon on either side. From Jerry's point of view, the grass was short, tough, and sparse. It looked golden beige under a big blue sky, the kind of color that makes the land look dry even when it isn't.

Then he crossed the border into Montana. The land opened wide, and the sky with it. This was Big Sky Country. The grass stayed low. The sky took over. Jerry felt small, like a cowboy from the Old West riding his horse across the endless landscape. In the distance, trains ran alongside the highway, sometimes long and slow, as if daring him to race them. He didn't.

Jerry began to see signs announcing he was nearing the Custer Battlefield Trading Post & Café and the Little Bighorn Battlefield, the place often called Custer's Last Stand.

Jerry remembered what he had read about the battle. In June 1876, Lt. Col. George Armstrong Custer led 210 men of the 7th Cavalry into the valley of the Little Bighorn, in what was probably the most lopsided battle in history. Waiting in the valley were an estimated 1,500 to 2,500 Lakota, Northern Cheyenne, and

Arapaho warriors, drawn together by leaders Sitting Bull and Crazy Horse. They were well-armed, many with repeating rifles, and they knew the ground.

In less than an hour, Custer and all 210 men were dead. Native losses were far lower. Estimates range from 40 to 100 killed, though exact numbers were never ascertained.

Jerry knew that was what history recorded. He also knew that the fallout of the battle had long-reaching consequences for the Native Americans.

The defeat shocked the nation and hardened it. Newspapers turned the fight into a legend overnight, a story of heroism and catastrophe that left no room for restraint. In Washington, fear translated into resolve.

Troops poured west. Treaties were brushed aside or rewritten. What had been one of the most significant Native American victories turned into an excuse for overwhelming force.

Within a few years, the resistance was broken, its leaders dead, imprisoned, or driven into exile. The battle came to stand for something larger—not triumph, but an ending. They won the fight, and it cost them the war. It was the opening shot in the final chapter of Plains Wars and the way of life for the Plains Indians.

Jerry could identify with the Native Americans. Custer had broken many treaties with them. How many times had he trusted someone only to be betrayed? That wasn't what got him and his men killed. It was his arrogance and bad judgment.

Jerry decided to stop by and see the place. He paid the park entrance fee and parked his bike near the visitor center. As Jerry dismounted, he had the strange feeling of dismounting a horse. He took off his helmet and noticed the place had a quiet reverence. No one spoke loudly, if at all. The only sound came from the American flag near the national cemetery, fluttering in the breeze.

As he walked uphill on the concrete path, the ground rose gently but steadily. The hill was exposed, open to the sky, with nothing to break the quiet except the soft rasp of wind moving through weeds and brittle stems.

The slope was dotted with short, unevenly spaced white markers. Custer had deployed his troopers in skirmish lines, each marker now standing where one of the first men had fallen.

Then a black iron fence in a large square traced the curve of the hill, guiding the eye upward toward the crest. This place marked where Custer and his men stood, fought, and died. Near the top, a stone monument stood, solid and mute.

Once at the top of the hill, he got a better look at the monument. The monument rose straight and pale against the open sky, its stacked stone sections narrowing slightly as they climbed upward. Sunlight struck the smooth faces of the stone, turning the engraved names of each fallen trooper into faint but deliberate script.

Jerry paused and read some of the names. Then he moved to the iron fence and looked inside at the white headstones. The markers were close together here, short, pale slabs rising unevenly from the earth, some straight, some tilted, all weathered by time. They formed no clean rows. Instead, they followed the shape of the land, scattered as if dictated by where people had fallen. There in the middle, marked in white letters on a black background, was Custer's marker.

Custer's remains were interred at West Point, and his men were buried in Custer National Cemetery. Jerry had seen the cemetery when he parked.

The irony of this was not lost on Jerry. His men are buried in a cemetery named after the man who led them to their deaths. Even in death, these guys just couldn't catch a break.

Jerry looked beyond the markers as the land opened wide and empty, stretching out into shallow valleys and distant ridges. He looked down on the Big Horn River and the place where the Native Americans had encamped. The banks of the river were covered in trees.

Custer didn't stand a chance. The Indians swept out from their encampments and overwhelmed him. Custer was surrounded and attacked from all sides.

A gust of wind swept across the ridge. For a moment, Jerry thought he heard the Lakota and Cheyenne war cries. He paused as the wind died down. Wasn't he doing the same thing as Custer? Convinced he was right to pursue Mark's death, yet with no clue who did it or why it had happened. What was he going to do? Charge in and take control?

This is different, Jerry thought, but he couldn't say why. He pushed the thought out of his head and headed back to his bike.

Jerry thought, *This is different. I know what I'm doing.*

Then a small voice in his head said, *But isn't that what addicts say?*

He started his bike and let the engine drown out his thoughts. He put on his helmet and headed out of the park.

Roughly 2,000 miles east of Jerry, at a private airstrip in the Adirondack Mountains, a military gray colored C-130J Hercules was loading up. On the side of the aircraft, the letters WE CARE were stenciled in four-foot-high letters.

Sam, Alex, Greg, and Mike, all wearing jeans and polo shirts, sunglasses, and ball caps, boarded the aircraft via the ramp. They sat down in the cargo net seats. Two pallets of black boxes were strapped to the plane's deck with cargo netting. Stenciled in white on the sides of the boxes were the words "Golden Fleece Pictures."

Half Blackjack Garret checked to make sure they were all strapped in, then gave the signal to raise the ramp.

WE CARE was the humanitarian arm of PROACTIVE, standing for Worldwide Endeavor, Care, Assistance, Relief, and Evacuation. The motto was "Where Compassion Meets Precision. We Go Where Others Can't"

The organization was headed by Half Blackjack Garrett. He had given it a different, non-public meaning for the name.

Wartime Extraction, Covert Assault, Recovery, and Evacuation. "We will never leave our people behind."

The sound of the four turboprop engines grew louder. Garrett made his way to the cockpit. The C-130J rolled onto the runway and held while the engines came up to power, the four turboprops flattening their blades and biting into the air. The brakes released, and the aircraft began to move heavily at first, then faster, the vibration settled into a steady hum. The loadmaster watched the gauges as the nose lifted slightly, not dramatically, but just enough. At rotation speed, the pilot eased back, the runway dropped away, and the aircraft climbed shallow and controlled, gear coming up as soon as there was clearance. It didn't leap into the sky. It pushed itself off the ground and kept going.

Once the plane had reached its cruising altitude, Garrett came from the flight deck. Sam stood up and stripped off her polo shirt. Underneath, she wore a black tank top that read "Got Indie?" Everyone else unbuckled their seatbelts, stood, and stretched. Sam stood at one end of the black boxes.

Garrett waved everyone forward to the door leading to the flight deck. Sam led the way. Once inside, Greg closed the door. The roar of the engines was reduced to a low hum. The space was just big enough for the five of them to stand in and face each other.

Greg looked around the space. He saw a small galley and a table to sit at. There was a door at the other end that led to the flight deck.

"Nice touch," he said.

"Thanks. I had it modified last year. I thought having a place to think on long missions might be nice," Garrett responded.

He turned to Sam. "What do you have for us, mission commander?"

"Thanks, Garrett," Sam said, stepping forward slightly.

"What we know right now is that Jerry found his friend Mark dead in the Badlands. He went to Deadwood to follow a clue and is now acting as a courier for an outlaw biker gang called "The Cowboys," whose leader is Johnny Ringo. Jerry is currently on his way to pick up a large amount of cash from an emissary of a gang called the Buckskin Raiders at the Norris Geyser Basin in Yellowstone National Park. From there, he is to go to Moab, pick up a package of printing plates, and then deliver them to Tombstone. Greg, what can you tell us about the Cowboys and Johnny Ringo?"

"The Cowboys weren't built," Greg said. "They were bought."

Mike shifted. "Bought how?"

"Johnny Ringo picked them up from a boutique club that already controlled a strip of old routes, middle of Arizona, down to the border. The same trails smugglers have been using since the seventies."

"And that's supposed to matter?" Alex asked.

"It doesn't," Greg said. "That's the point. Every agency knows those routes. Cameras, sensors, aerials. They're burned. No serious outfit touches them anymore."

"So why keep them?"

"Because Johnny needs a gang," Greg said. "And because the Cowboys don't know they're holding dead ground."

A pause.

"From law enforcement and other sources, this is what I've pieced together. Most of them are wannabes," Greg went on. "Guys who couldn't patch into bigger clubs. Some washed out. Some never even got close. Johnny keeps the image tight, talks about legacy, tradition, territory. Makes it sound like they're sitting on something historic."

"And they buy it?" Sam asked.

"They're grateful to belong," Greg said. "That's the leverage. He gives them a name, a patch, a story. In return, they don't ask questions."

Garrett stepped forward. "So they're not a real threat."

Greg shook his head. "They're not smart, and they're not respected. But they're loyal. And when someone like Johnny Ringo is the one writing the story, that's enough to make them dangerous."

"Any background on this Johnny Ringo?" Garrett asked.

"Other than the same name as the outlaw, not much. It was like he appeared out of the desert a few years ago when he bought the gang. We are still digging," Greg said.

"Now what?" Mike asked.

Sam spoke. "We are going to Tombstone to cover Jerry. He seems to think there is some connection to his friend's death."

"What if there is?" Alex said.

Sam turned to her sister. "Then we keep him from doing something stupid."

"He's a trained agent," Mike said.

Sam looked at Mike. "Yes, but this was his friend, an innocent bystander. Control is sending us to protect Jerry from himself."

"There would be no use in recalling him. He would quit and pursue his hunch anyway," Greg added.

"Control feels that if he is onto something, then it might lead to something bigger. He will need backup," Sam said.

Everyone nodded.

Sam looked around the room. "Let's review the cover story."

"Golden Fleece Pictures is an independent production collective developing *The Long Return,* a Western film exploring what remains after violence becomes legend," everyone said in unison.

Sam smiled. "You've been practicing."

"Yes, I practiced especially hard," Mike said with a smile.

"Why did you pick Golden Fleece Pictures?" Garrett asked.

"Argo was a real Cold War–era extraction mission where CIA intelligence officers used a fake film production as cover to move people out of Iran. The company name was deliberately boring, and the movie itself didn't matter. Only that the story was believable. The name of Jason's ship in Jason and the Argonauts was Argo. They were looking for the golden fleece. I chose Golden Fleece Pictures as a nod to that idea.

"All right, now for cover stories. I'll go first and then around the room," Sam said.

She took a breath. "My name is Samantha Soska, or Sam for short. I'm the producer of *The Long Return.* My job is to see if this movie is even possible. I'm responsible for permits, locations, schedules, and budgets. I'm the one people talk to if they have questions or concerns. If anything changes, it's because production is still figuring itself out."

She looked at her sister.

"I'm Alexandra, or Alex for short. I'm here as the on-set medic. Low-budget or not, desert locations mean heat, dehydration, and liability. I keep an eye on everyone, handle first aid, and make sure we don't do anything that gets the production shut down."

Alex looked at Garrett.

"I'm Garrett Johns. I'm directing the project. I'm scouting light, space, and atmosphere, trying to understand how the town feels when nothing's happening. I'll probably visit the same places a lot. That's just me working things out visually."

Sam looked at Mike and nodded.

"Name's Michael Stephens, but everybody calls me Mike. I'm doing location sound and ambient recording. Things like footsteps, wind, room tone, background noise, stuff people don't think about but make or break a quiet film. I'll mostly be listening, not talking."

"I want to see that happen," Greg said with a grin.

"And you would be good, sir," Mike shot back, feigning offense.

"I'm the production manager, Gregory St. George, or as my boss Sam calls me, Greg. I handle logistics, transport, lodging, schedules, and gear. If we're late, early, stuck, or suddenly leaving, that's on me. My job is to keep things moving smoothly so everyone else can focus on the work."

"Speaking of gear, what do we have in the boxes?" Sam asked.

"Lights, digital cameras, mics, sound booms, makeup, field medic kit, and other odds and ends an indie film team would have. Also, enough firepower to get us out of any confrontations if they might occur. We can go over the inventory before we land and pick up anything we need on the way down to Tombstone," Greg explained.

"We will land in Tucson and pick up a motorhome and an SUV for the trip.

We will be staying at the Wells Fargo RV Park. It is between Freemont and Allen streets. You should be able to hear the shootout at the O.K. Corral from there," Garrett said.

He looked at his watch. "We land in about five hours."

"All right, everybody, try to get some rest," Sam said, turning. "Greg, let's go through the inventory."

CHAPTER 13

Jerry's phone alarm went off at 4 a.m. The sky was beginning to lighten. He had spent the night in one of the cabins at an RV park in Livingston, Montana. Jerry swung his legs out of bed and stretched. His body ached from yesterday's long ride.

He looked at the time. Jerry had only two hours until the 6 a.m. delivery at Norris Geyser Basin. It would take at least an hour and a half to get there. He hurriedly packed his things and left. He had checked the map five times the night before to make sure he had the right route. Johnny had given specific instructions as to where Colt's man was supposed to be waiting.

Jerry was grateful that traffic was extremely light this morning. Forty-five minutes later, he passed under the Roosevelt Arch at the North Entrance to Yellowstone National Park. He knew he only had forty miles to go. He paid his entry fee at the gate. The maximum speed limit inside the park was forty miles per hour, and even slower in some places. He pulled over for a moment to put his helmet in his saddlebag and put on his skull cap and goggles.

He would follow the Grand Loop Road south. Jerry was captivated by the place's natural beauty. He rode past Mammoth Hot Springs, which didn't look like a typical geothermal area. He thought it looked constructed, almost architectural. Tier after tier of white and pale gold terraces rose up the hillside, frozen in motion like cascading stone waterfalls. The surfaces were ribbed and scalloped, some smooth, some rough, catching the early light so they glowed softly rather than shone.

Thin sheets of steam drifted off the formations. Water moved slowly here, trickling and leaving dark wet lines that stained the terraces in rust, gray, and faint green. Jerry caught a faint whiff of minerals and sulfur. Someday he would come back to see it, but he had to press on.

The light changed quickly. Long shadows stretched across the road as it wound through open valleys and stands of lodgepole pine. Jerry heard birds before he saw them. Their sharp calls cut through the low rumble of the engine. Wisps of ground fog sat in the low spots, briefly swallowing the road before he passed through them.

Bison appeared without warning. A dark shape near the shoulder turned into a massive animal standing still, steam lifting from its back in the cold morning air. He slowed as he eased past. The last thing he needed was a confrontation with an animal that was twice the weight and size of he and the bike combined. If Jerry saw one, he was pretty sure it wasn't alone. He would give the animal the respect it deserved. The smell of grass and wet soil grew stronger as the land flattened. The smell of pine filled the air. The road tightened into gentle climbs and sweeping turns.

As Jerry approached Norris Geyser Basin, the landscape changed subtly but decisively. The clean scent of pine gave way to stronger sulfur. Steam vents hissed and sighed in the distance, audible even over the bike. The ground looked lighter here, chalky, almost fragile. To Jerry, it looked like the crust of an apple pie in places. Plumes of vapor rose steadily into the cool air, glowing in the early sun. He turned into the almost deserted parking lot of the basin and rolled to a stop. Jerry cut off the engine.

Suddenly, it was quiet again, except for the low rumble of steam escaping the earth somewhere. He looked around and saw that the parking lot was divided by a thin stand of pine trees. Jerry could see an RV and another car parked on the other side.

Then the silence was broken when he heard the roar of a motorcycle coming from the other side. At first, he couldn't see because some of the trees blocked his view. As the rider passed, Jerry caught sight of a chopper with a long frame and a low seat. Its rider was a white man in his late thirties or early forties, tall and lean, with a thin rather than muscular build.

One thing that caught Jerry's eye was the man's short black hair and trimmed beard. Jerry watched as the man rode off at a steady speed, didn't weave or look back, and appeared calm and deliberate as he left.

Jerry thought that was a little odd. He looked around, and other than him, he didn't see any other motorcycles. Jerry shrugged and dismounted his bike. He put the goggles and skull cap in his saddlebag. He unzipped his leather jacket and walked to the trailhead for the basin.

As Jerry got closer, he could hear the roar of the many geysers in the basin. He walked under the archway of the closed Norris Geyser Basin Museum and down the steps leading to the path that would take him to the basin. There was no one around as he walked. His footsteps sounded loud on the wooden slatted path. He passed a trail to his right that headed south, then continued to the basin.

Jerry took a moment to look at the basin before he turned north. The scene was surreal. Steam rose in low, drifting plumes from hot springs and vents scattered across the flat ground, creating a hazy layer just above the surface. Shallow streams of hot water had cut winding paths through the basin, their surfaces caught the sunlight and flashed silver as they flowed.

The ground was dry and gritty, its color a muted mix of browns and grays, with patches of mineral crust where water had evaporated. Small, stunted shrubs and young pines dotted the foreground, spaced far apart, underscoring how harsh the environment was. Pools of bright aqua green dotted the basin. In the distance, a darker band of evergreen forest lined the horizon, standing in contrast to the open, exposed basin. Steam rose and drifted, suggesting steady heat just beneath the surface. The low rumble of steam from vents was everywhere.

Jerry had read somewhere that Yellowstone was, or still is, an active super volcano. From his viewpoint, he believed it. He turned north and took the wooden boardwalk that curved gently to the right, elevated just above the ground, guiding Jerry safely across the basin. The land itself looked raw and unsettled, with dark soil, crusted mineral patches, and sparse vegetation. A line of trees formed a low boundary in the distance. The steam softened the horizon, giving the scene a hazy, breathing quality, as if the ground itself was slowly exhaling beneath the open sky.

After a few minutes, he was almost at the top of the north side of the basin. Jerry could see the trail he was supposed to take leading off to the right. He took one last look at the basin. It was spread across a gently sloping landscape under a clear blue sky. Dozens of steam plumes rose from vents and pools scattered across pale green, red, rust, and blue-stained ground, giving the scene a constant sense of motion. Where heat and minerals had stripped the soil, the earth was cracked and uneven, which created layers in muted colors of grays, tans, rust, and faint yellows.

Shallow pools and wet patches reflected light in irregular shapes, while steam drifted sideways in the breeze, partially obscuring the terrain behind it. What a sight, Jerry thought. He wasn't sure if God existed, but he was sure of one thing - no man could have created what he saw.

Jerry turned onto the trail leading away from the basin. He checked the time, as he passed Huphar Lake. If Johnny's directions were correct, he had only a few hundred yards to go. He checked the time again. He was five minutes early. Jerry kept walking up the slightly sloping path where he was supposed to see a large rock. A few steps later, it came into view. A rock was an understatement. It was a boulder the size of a city bus. Jerry stopped, looked around for prying eyes, and listened for signs of human activity.

After a few minutes, he cautiously approached the boulder, careful not to step on any branches on the forest floor. He reached the rock and stopped again to listen. Still, he heard nothing except the wind in the trees and a bird calling in the distance. Jerry crept around the rock slowly. Then, as he was about to be on the opposite side, he saw a pair of motorcycle boots with the toes up and soles facing out, like someone was sitting just around the corner.

He moved even more slowly. Then, the rest of the figure was revealed as a massive man with long hair pulled back in a ponytail. The man sat with his back against a massive boulder, its shadow swallowing half his body. His faded blue jeans clung to unmoving legs. A denim cut lay open over his chest, the fabric sun-bleached, its edges frayed as if it had seen too many miles. The man's face tilted slightly to one side, with a slack jaw, and eyes half-closed. Jerry noticed the man was seated in a large pool of blood, already soaking into the pine needles and dirt. Jerry checked the man's pulse just to confirm what he already knew. The man was dead.

Jerry looked around the ground, but it wasn't disturbed as if there had been a struggle. Not far from the man was a bundle wrapped in a bandana. Jerry opened it and found a stack of cash. He looked closer at the man's coat. On a narrow strip on the left side was the name "Mango". On the right side was a patch stitched "Sergeant-at-Arms."

Jerry's head was spinning. He looked around to see if anyone was watching. He knew the coat was evidence that Mango had been set up before he ever knew it, and until Jerry could trace where it was supposed to go, it didn't belong back in circulation. He meant to return it to Colt's people once the truth was clear, but not until he was sure the same play wasn't being run on him.

He pulled the man forward to remove his cut. The body toppled to the side. That's when Jerry saw the switchblade knife buried in the man's back, just below the rib cage. Amazingly, the blood had flowed down without staining the coat. After a few minutes, Jerry managed to remove the coat and fold it into the smallest square he could. Mango had been a large man.

He heard voices approaching coming up the path. Jerry retreated into the woods and hid behind some brush. He saw the pointed crest of two park ranger hats disappearing and reappearing as they passed trees, coming up the path about a hundred yards away.

This is going to look great. I have a bundle of cash and a denim vest. There is a dead body, less than twenty yards from me. I'm not only going back to prison, but I'm also going to the electric chair, Jerry thought.

Jerry unconsciously held his breath as they came into full view. Revealing a tall, thin male in his late fifties and a young, lanky female. Both wore a tan flat-brimmed campaign hat with the National Park Service arrowhead emblem, a neatly pressed gray shirt, green trousers, sturdy brown boots, and a black leather duty belt. They were engaged in a mundane exchange about work. Start times, end times, and what each planned to do at the end of the day. They didn't even look over at the boulder hiding the body on the other side. If they stopped and looked back, they would see the body.

As Jerry watched them pass and walk further away, time just seemed to stop. He saw them moving, but it appeared to him as if they didn't move, like they were walking in place. Then he suddenly exhaled. It sounded to Jerry like the rush of wind. This close, they must have heard him exhale. His eyes were still fixed on the pair. Nothing happened as they finally disappeared around a bend in the trail.

Jerry waited a few more minutes before standing. He looked around to get his bearings. He knew he couldn't go back the way he came. He would make his way through the woods, skirting Nuphar Lake. Then he followed the road back to the parking lot, making sure to stay well within the tree line so he wouldn't be seen. It would take time, but he really couldn't think of another way to go.

He started off knowing he had to be careful not to break through the topsoil and fall into a sinkhole or a steam vent. As he went, another thought came to mind. That would be running into wildlife. His fear of being caught with a bundle of money and a dead man's coat dissipated. Jerry had a vision of a large bear emerging from nowhere. He chose his steps carefully, but moved a little quicker.

By the time Jerry made it back to the parking lot after an hour and a half, it was filling up. There were other motorcycles parked in a few spaces, as well. During his journey, he had wrapped the money into the cut. He tucked it under his arm and confidently walked to his bike. Jerry remembered to act like you owned the place, and people won't question you.

No one stopped him and no one took notice of him. On his bike, he stowed the bundle in one of his saddlebags and put on his skull cap and goggles. He started his bike and rode out of the parking lot. Once he reached the Grand Loop Road, he turned right to keep heading south.

Jerry went through the route to Moab, Utah, in his head. The fastest way out of the park would be out the West Yellowstone gate. He would follow U.S. 20 through Idaho, head south on I-15 at Idaho Falls, then take U.S. 6 East to U.S. 191 into Moab. It would take him about fourteen hours of road time. Jerry would ride as far as he could until he had to rest. He looked forward to the time. There was a lot to think about.

CHAPTER 14

Jerry was eight hours into his ride to Moab. He had just crossed the Utah State line when Sam walked into Johnny Ringo's Bar on South 10th Street in Tombstone.

The double front doors faced 10th Street. The late-afternoon sun was blocked by low buildings across the street, but it was bright enough to stream into the bar. The air conditioning felt good after Sam had been in the mid-July sun.

Sam wore a lightweight long-sleeve white blouse over dark blue Capri pants and dusty black Sketchers. She wore black oversized sunglasses, and her hair was pulled back in a ponytail. On her head was a black baseball cap with the words "Golden Fleece Pictures" embroidered in gold thread.

She pulled up her sunglasses and let her eyes adjust to the interior lighting. She looked around. The room was wide and open, with polished floors and round, high-top tables, each surrounded by metal barstools. A pool table sat on the right. The bar ran along the left wall, well stocked with bottles. The walls were crowded with framed photos, beer signs, and memorabilia.

Off to the right corner, there was a setup for a band. Sam went to the bar and sat on a barstool. The bartender, an old man with a gray handlebar mustache and a warm smile, came over to her. His hair was cropped short, and he wore a blue Western pearl button shirt and jeans.

"What would you like to drink?" he asked.

"I'll have a draft beer," Sam said.

"Yes, ma'am."

He pulled a glass off the back of the bar and filled it from a tap. He placed a coaster in front of Sam and set the beer on it.

"Do you want to open a tab?" the man asked.

Sam reached into her pocket, pulled out a $20 bill, and handed it to him.

"How much?"

"Three dollars during happy hour. Then $4 after that."

"When I'm done with the twenty, let me know. Keep a dollar for yourself every time I order," Sam explained.

The man smiled. "Yes, ma'am. We have karaoke tonight. It starts at seven. You might want to stay for it."

Sam looked at the clock behind the bar. The time was 5 p.m.

She looked back at him and said, "Maybe."

She took her hat off, set it on the bar, and took a sip of her beer. It went down surprisingly easily and tasted good. The kind of good that makes you want more. But Sam knew she had to be careful. It would be easy to just stay at the bar and forget for a while.

A few minutes later, Sam heard the front door open. She didn't get a clear look at who came in because of the sun's glare. When the door closed, she saw it was a curvy woman.

Her black hair was pulled into a ponytail. She wore a white sleeveless blouse with the top two buttons open, form-fitting jeans, and black polished cowboy boots. She also wore a pair of oversized dark glasses. The woman took a seat on a barstool two places over from Sam, leaving an empty seat between the two. She took off her sunglasses and hung them in the "v" created in the front of her blouse. The bartender walked over to the woman.

"Hey, Lucy. What will it be?" he asked.

"Same as always, Bill," the woman said.

Her smooth, smoky voice fits her, Sam thought.

Bill brought her a pint of draft beer. She took a sip, set it down, and looked around at the almost empty bar.

"Excuse me," Sam said.

Lucia turned to Sam.

"I just wanted to say I like your outfit. It really works," Sam said.

A smile crept across Lucia's face. "Thank you for noticing."

"Where did you get your blouse and boots?" Sam asked.

"In the historic district on Allen Street at Spurs Western Wear," Lucia said.

Sam looked surprised. "I've been up and down Allen Street all day and missed it. I'll have to look for it."

"They have a great selection of Western wear, and the prices are decent," Lucia said.

"Thanks. Oh, where are my manners? I'm Samantha, or Sam for short," Sam said, holding out her hand.

Lucia leaned over and shook Sam's hand. "Lucia, but you can call me Lucy."

"Are you local?" Sam asked.

"Ha! No, I should be as many times as I've come here," Lucia said. "What brings you here?"

Sam turned the ball cap on the counter to show the production company's name.

"I'm a movie producer. I'm here scouting for an indie movie."

"What's it about?" Lucia asked. She appeared genuinely interested.

"It's called *The Long Return*, a Western exploring what remains after violence becomes legend."

That made Lucia pause and look away. Sam could see that she was lost in thought.

What remains after violence becomes legend? What had happened to her after the violence she had witnessed? More to the point, what would happen to her? Johnny's operation isn't sustainable, and to be honest, neither is he, Lucia thought.

Lucia felt something shift inside her. Just a feeling. It wasn't a huge change, but it was the beginning of something. She shook her head slightly and turned back to Sam with a smile.

"Sorry about that. I had a thought about something else."

"No problem," Sam said, smiling.

Lucia couldn't remember the last time she'd had a friendly conversation with another woman in which the topic wasn't related to Johnny's business.

"How long will you be in town?"

"About a week. And you?" Sam asked.

"At least a few days until my boyfriend finishes a deal he is working on," Lucia answered.

"What kind of deal? If you don't mind me asking?" Sam asked.

"He brokers, manages, and supplies reenactors for historically accurate events tied to Tombstone's past, such as gunfights, trials, stagecoach robberies, territorial disputes, and anything else he can think of. He stays away from the famous stuff. He thinks there might be interest in lesser-known events across southern Arizona," Lucia explained, hoping it sounded convincing.

"Maybe I can use some of them in the movie if it gets made." Sam picked up her glass. "What should we toast to?"

"To new faces," Lucia said, raising her glass.

"And to good company," Sam added.

The women took a drink and set their glasses down.

"Next round's on me," Lucia said as he waved Bill over and ordered two more drinks. Bill poured two more drafts and set them before each woman.

Sam raised her glass to Lucia. "Thank you. Next one's on me."

The front door opened again. Sam smiled as she recognized the silhouette in the doorway, having seen it hundreds of times before. Sam knew the walk was more like a swagger. Lucia also turned to see who it was.

It was Mike wearing a tan cowboy hat and a light-colored, long-sleeved buttoned shirt with a high collar. The fabric had thin vertical stripes with small, repeating decorative patterns running down the front. The style looked old-fashioned and formal, similar to a late-1800s Western work shirt. He wore tan pants and brown Ariat boots.

Mike tipped his hat to Lucia. "Ma'am," he said as he went by and took a seat on the other side of Sam.

Lucia made a genuine smile at the recognition. Bill, the bartender, walked up to Mike.

"What will it be?"

"How about a bourbon and Coke on the rocks?" Mike asked.

"Coming right up," Bill said and began to make the drink.

Mike turned to Sam. "I'll be right back. I've got to talk to a man about a horse."

Bill saw Mike look around, then point. "Men's room is over there."

"Thanks," Mike said as he headed toward the back of the room.

"Who's he?" Lucia said with a smile.

Sam's head snapped toward Lucia. "What?"

Lucia leaned back slightly, holding her hands up. "I didn't mean to cut in."

Sam realized how she had reacted and relaxed. She flashed a smile.

"Oh, sorry, I was thinking of something else."

Sam jerked her thumb back toward where Mike had gone. "Him? Oh, no, he's my sound engineer. It's strictly professional between us."

"Too bad. You two would make a good-looking couple," Lucia said.

She noticed Sam blush at the idea.

"Thank you, but family and kids aren't in the cards for me," Sam said.

"Why?"

"My job takes me to a lot of places. I couldn't give my family the attention I believe they deserve," Sam explained.

Lucia nodded her head in understanding.

"What about you? Any plans with the boyfriend?" Sam asked.

Lucia sighed. "I don't think he's the marrying kind."

Mike came back to the bar as Bill set the drink down in front of him. Mike reached into his pocket. Sam held her hand up.

"I think the boss can buy you a drink," she said.

"Thank you, thank you very much," Mike said in his best Elvis impersonation.

"That's pretty good," Lucia said.

Mike smiled. "I'd say it again, but I don't want to sound redundant."

Lucia giggled and looked at Sam. "You really need to think about your life choices."

Mike gave her a puzzled look.

Sam jumped off her barstool and looked at Mike. "Hey, why don't we play a few games of pool?"

She waved Bill over. "Can you give me $5 in quarters. Please?"

Bill nodded, went to the register, brought back a roll of quarters, and handed them to her. She took her beer and Mike his drink, and they headed for the pool table.

Lucia watched as Sam and Mike went to the pool table. Mike walked over to the electronic jukebox on the wall, dropped some bills in, and selected a few songs. The first lines of "Simple Man" by Lynyrd Skynyrd started as he walked back to the pool table. Sam was already lining up to take the first shot with her pool stick.

Lucia didn't care what Sam had said. They sure looked like a couple. It was in how they interacted with each other. The light touches, the knowing looks. The way Mike looked at her, the seductive way she bent over the table to take her shot.

Sam took her shot and turned away from Lucia toward Mike. The music was just loud enough to cover their conversation.

She smiled and said in a low tone, "What's everyone else doing?"

Mike circled the table looking for a good angle. Once he was back, he tapped his stick on the table.

"Getting the lay of the land. Greg is touring the Good Enough Silver Mine. Alex is taking a tour of The Bird Cage, and Garrett's back at the RV keeping watch of the gear. Greg says Jerry's at least two days away."

Sam smiled and nodded as Mike took his shot and made it. They moved around the table as if choreographed. Mike lined up his shot and looked up at Sam.

"Who's the woman?"

"Don't know exactly. Her name is Lucia, but she goes by Lucy. She's a regular, but not a local. Her boyfriend has some type of cosplay company. She thinks we should be a couple," Sam explained.

"She sure is a pretty one," Mike said.

Sam nodded in agreement. "Yes, she is."

Mike missed his shot and moved out of the way for Sam. "Kept woman?"

Sam gave Mike a slight grin. "What do you think?"

"Does she have a job? I get the feeling that with the way she looks, she doesn't need a job," Mike said.

Sam nodded as she leaned over to take her shot. She missed. Mike picked up some chalk and circled the table as he chalked his stick. He stopped and leaned over, looked up at Sam.

"What's the plan?" he asked.

Sam gave a furtive glance toward Lucia, who had turned back to the bar.

"I don't know yet. Let's wait and see what the others find out."

As they continued to play, more people arrived. A waitress, dressed in denim shorts and a sleeveless blouse, placed signs that read "RESERVED" on a few of the tables.

The waitress came over to Sam and Mike. "Can I get you two anything?"

Mike grinned at the button the woman wore that read: "Tip Me or Die of Thirst."

Can't blame her for being direct, Mike thought.

"Two draft beers, please," Mike said.

The woman smiled and headed to the bar.

While Sam lined up her shot to start another game, Mike watched as a man in his early forties entered the bar.

He sported a fading blond Mohawk and was dressed like a man who'd lost a bet with the Eighties. The outfit was completed with lime-green snakeskin pants, a black mesh tank top, and a silver jacket.

Bill the bartender waved to him as he dragged two rectangular, battered flight cases behind him. He began setting up his equipment, which included speakers on tripods and a flat-screen TV aimed at an open area that looked like a dance floor. Then he set his laptop on a small collapsible table. He taped down extension cords and cables with black gaffer tape. The last thing he did was get the mics lined up, tip jar out, and ready to hand the mic over to anyone brave enough to sing. He then unplugged the jukebox.

He did a mic check. His voice was deep and rich, just like a DJ's should sound.

"Check, check, check, check. Hello, everyone, I'm Rex "Neon" Calder, the greatest thing to come out of the Eighties. I'll kick the fires and light the tires in about fifteen minutes."

There were some groans and applause from the gathering crowd.

Mike looked back at the bar and saw a man about six feet tall, with slicked-back dark hair, his back turned to Mike, standing next to Lucia. They were engaged in conversation. The man was wearing a black Western shirt with white piping, jeans, and cowboy boots.

Mike leaned over to Sam. "I think your new friend has company."

Sam looked over, then back at Mike. "I think that's the boyfriend."

Just as she finished saying that, Lucia and the man started to walk over to them. Mike could see that the man had a neatly trimmed mustache that sharpened his defined jaw, and pale gray eyes

Mike turned to Sam and calmly said, "I think we have company."

Lucia led the way. One thing Sam noticed was that the couple didn't seem like a couple. Something was off. It felt more like she was watching business partners than a relationship. They reached the pool table.

"This is Sam and Mike. They are here to make a movie or something," Lucia said and continued, "this is Johnny Ringo, my boyfriend."

Mike smiled and held out his hand to Johnny. "I'm Mike. You own the bar?"

There was an awkward pause, and then Johnny smiled and shook Mike's hand. Johnny's handshake was a cross between a too-long grip and a bone crusher. This guy had issues with dominance and strength. Something else Mike noticed was his smile. It reminded him of an officer he knew in the Army who smiled like Johnny. His mouth smiled, but the rest of his face didn't. There was something behind those eyes, but Mike was pretty sure it wasn't anything good.

"Would you like to join us at our private table?" Johnny asked.

Mike looked at Sam. She nodded.

"Sure," Mike said.

The bar was now full of people. Johnny led the way to a reserved table near the front by the dance floor. Mike took a seat where he could face the door. Johnny didn't appear to care as he took the seat opposite. Sam sat to the right of Mike, closest to the dance floor. Lucia took the one opposite Sam.

Rex stepped onto the dance floor, holding a mic. "Good evening. I'll start tonight's show with a few oldies but goodies. Once you've had enough drinks and get tired of me, you'll want to sing."

He looked around the crowd and saw Lucia. "I see we have la voz de un angel in the house tonight."

Sam leaned over and whispered in Mike's ear. "She has the voice of an angel. Also, I need to let the team know what's going on."

Mike nodded. Sam stood up.

"Before things get too crazy, I need to powder my nose."

She headed to the ladies' room and found an empty stall. Sam could hear the muffled sound of Rex singing. She closed the door, pulled out her cellphone, sat down on the commode, and tapped out a message to meet at Johnny Ringo's Bar. Alex, Greg, and Garrett acknowledged. Greg sent a second message that he would relieve Garrett, because the bar scene wasn't his thing. Sam agreed and headed back to the table.

After a few songs, people started lining up to sing. Some were good, others probably sounded better in the shower, because the water drowned out most of their singing.

Johnny sat at the table like a peacock and drank like a fish. He leaned forward toward Mike.

He pointed at Lucia. "She's the best singer in this place."

"I'm sure she is," Mike said.

Sam saw Alex enter the bar and head toward the back. Alex wore a red wig under a battered cowboy hat, and a long-sleeved tan blouse over jeans and tennis shoes. A moment later, Garrett entered and went to the bar. He wore a black T-shirt, jeans, and black work boots.

Johnny looked at Lucia.

"I think you need to prove it," he said with a slight slur.

Sam picked up on Lucia's awkward position. She reached her hand out to touch Lucia.

"There are a lot of people who want to sing. Maybe in a little while," Sam said.

Lucia nodded, and Sam stood up again. "I might need to slow down. I need to go again."

Sam headed to the ladies' room. Alex followed in a roundabout way. Once inside, they found themselves alone. They looked in the mirror and checked their hair.

"We are sitting with Johnny Ringo and his girlfriend," Sam said as she brushed her hair back with her hands.

Alex turned to her sister. "First impressions?"

"He is arrogant, overbearing. Her name is Lucia. She has a great singing voice, apparently, but she is definitely a kept woman," Sam said.

"What do you want us to do?"

"Find Garrett and act like a bar couple and cover us. Ringo's beginning to get drunk, and I don't know how he's going to act."

There was a commotion outside the door. Two women came in chatting incessantly. Alex nodded in the mirror and left the room. The two women each entered their own empty stall and closed the door. Still chatting away.

Sam took a deep breath as she looked at herself in the mirror. *This Johnny Ringo guy is not what I expected. The thing to do is get more information about him,* Sam thought.

She checked herself one last time and then paused and stared at herself as a thought crossed her mind.

Wait a minute. Lucia said this guy has a company that does reenactments and cosplay. I can use that.

A smile crossed her face. She gave herself a wink and left. The karaoke had taken a break, and the dance floor was full of people dancing to a slow country song. Sam made her way through the crowd to the table. Johnny, Lucia, and Mike seemed frozen, watching the people dance.

Mike smiled as Sam approached. He stood up.

"Wanna dance?"

Sam smiled. "Why yes."

She wrapped her arms around his neck, and he held her by the waist, and they slowly moved away from the table.

Mike looked down at Sam. "We haven't done this in a long time."

She blushed, turned away, then came back. "Let's focus on the mission."

"You are correct," Mike smiled.

She leaned her head on his shoulder. "What happened while I was gone?"

Mike leaned into her. "He doesn't talk much. I tried to find some common ground, but no luck."

As they danced, Mike saw Garrett and Alex dancing together across the room.

"I have something to talk about. Just follow my lead," Sam said.

The song faded. Sam and Mike came back to take their seats at the table.

Rex picked up his mic again and looked around the room. "Who's next?"

No one came forward. Mike suddenly stood up and walked up to Rex.

"Hey, cowboy, what are you looking to sing?" Rex asked.

"How about 'Hound Dog' by the King?" Mike asked.

Rex grinned and handed over the mic. Mike did a little shiver and stretched his arms to get into character.

Mike belted out the first line of Hound Dog loud and unmistakable. His impersonation was so good that, for a second, it sounded like Elvis himself had entered the bar.

Johnny Ringo looked up from his drink.

Mike didn't stay planted at the microphone. He swung his hips. His singing was confident and precise. Mike looked around the room. The crowd responded with claps and whistles.

Mike was enjoying his own performance. Johnny didn't look away. His expression stayed flat, but his jaw tightened as the lyrics rolled on, line after line, impossible to miss. When the song ended and the applause started, Johnny's drink was untouched.

Rex took the microphone from Mike and looked at the crowd.

"I think Elvis is in the building."

The crowd applauded again. Mike bowed and walked back to his seat.

"That was really good," Lucia said.

"Thank you," Mike responded.

Johnny looked at Lucia. "Time to show them what you got."

Lucia smiled, stood up, and walked to Rex. The crowd cheered as she took the mic and nodded to Rex.

She started the Fleetwood Mac song "Dreams" quietly. Her voice was steady and clear, with a comfortable pitch and no strain. She kept the tempo relaxed and let the words come out naturally.

She moved to the center of the floor. Someone lowered the house lights, and Rex turned a soft white light on her, putting her into a half shadow.

As the song went on, she opened her voice just enough to show her range, holding a few notes longer and smoothing the transitions between lines.

She stood mostly still, focused on the microphone. By the chorus, the room had gone quiet. When she finished, there was a short pause before the applause started.

She handed the mic back to Rex. As the lights came back up, and before she could get back to her chair, someone in the bar yelled, "Duet!"

Then someone else yelled, "Duet!"

Then it became a chant, "Duet, duet, duet, duet, duet.'

Rex grinned. He waved Mike forward. "You heard 'em, Elvis. Let's have some fun."

"Lucy, are you game?" Rex asked.

She looked at Johnny, who nodded with approval. Lucia stepped forward. Whistles and shouts came from the crowd.

"I've got one that I think everyone knows," Rex said as he handed a microphone to the pair.

The opening bars to Bonnie Raitt's "Something to Talk About" played as couples took to the dance floor.

Lucia started to sing, "People are talkin'—"

The crowd responded instantly, "Talkin' 'bout people!"

Laughter rippled through the bar.

Lucia kept going, finishing the verse, brushing through the lines about whispers and rumors like they didn't matter. The crowd stayed with her, clapping in time, and hanging on every word.

Then Mike stepped forward. He waited just long enough for the room to notice.

He leaned into the mic and sang, "Laugh just a little—"

The crowd shouted back, louder than before, "Too loud!"

Mike grinned and finished the verse, stretching the words, letting the tone shift from playful to pointed.

Then Lucia moved back beside him.

They sang together. Their voices locked in as one: "Let's give 'em—"

The crowd roared the answer, shaking the room, "Something to talk about!"

Couples danced and fed off the moment. As the song rolled on, Lucia and Mike carried it easily, and the crowd chimed in whenever they could.

Johnny suddenly stood. Sam was startled as he grabbed her by the hand, firm and sudden, and pulled her onto the dance floor. He made sure to be right in front of Lucia and Mike. Sam went with it. Garrett noticed and led Alex to the dance floor and moved closer to Sam and Johnny.

As the song continued, Johnny drew Sam closer than necessary. One hand settled low. Possessive. Deliberate. A message meant for the stage. The duo kept their composure and finished the song.

The crowd rewarded them with a standing ovation. They bowed and waved as they took their seats. Sam and Johnny were waiting for them.

Sam smiled at them. "You two sounded great."

"Thank you," Lucia said.

"I've never done a duet to that song," Mike said with a grin.

"The crowd seemed to love it," Sam said.

Mike looked at Johnny. "What did you think?"

Johnny gave Mike his fake smile. "Not bad for an amateur."

Mike laughed. "Thanks. There's always room for improvement."

"Yeah, a lot of room." Johnny smiled.

Sam shot a sideways glance at Mike to see his reaction.

"I'll sign up for lessons when I get home," Mike said, keeping his composure.

Sam turned to Johnny. "Lucy tells me you have a company that does re-creation of events here in Tombstone and other places. We might need some actors for our movie."

Johnny's head snapped to look at Sam. He said nothing for a long moment. "Yeah, I do have some guys that do that."

He stood up, stretched, and looked at Lucia. "Speaking of work, we have to go. I have some things to do before the sun comes up."

Lucia stood up and smiled at Sam and Mike. "Nice to meet you."

"Nice to meet you," Mike and Sam responded in unison.

Lucia waved and followed Johnny out of the bar.

A moment later, Alex and Garrett came over to the table.

"Are these seats taken?" Garrett asked.

Mike gestured to a chair. "Only by you."

Alex and Garrett sat down.

"That's Johnny Ringo?" Garrett asked.

"In the flesh." Mike smiled.

"He looks like he's a piece of work," Alex remarked.

"I got a feeling Lucy is going to get an earful after tonight," Sam said.

"Let's head back to the RV and get some dinner," Mike suggested.

"Good idea. Mike and I will leave first, then you two. We'll go down Allen Street through the historic district. We will take the right side of the street, and Alex and Garrett will be on overwatch on the left side. When we get to the Oriental, we'll pause and let you move forward and be overwatch for you," Sam explained.

Mike and Sam left the bar. A few minutes later, Alex and Garrett followed. Mike and Sam made their way down East Allen Street toward the Tombstone Historic District. The night sky was clear and full of stars. The street was lit by a few streetlights, giving it a yellow-white haze. If it weren't for the seriousness of the mission, it would have been a pleasant evening for a walk through the historic district. They slowed down or stopped occasionally to make sure they weren't being followed by anyone with nefarious intent.

A few minutes behind them, Alex and Garrett started down the opposite side of the street. Close enough to cover Mike and Sam, but far enough not to look obvious. There weren't many people out this time of night, and, being the middle of July, it was the slow season for tourists.

Sam and Mike both knew this was good and bad. For the good guys, fewer people around meant fewer civilians to protect and fewer witnesses to complicate things, but it also meant nowhere to blend in and no help close by if something went wrong. For the bad guys, the quiet offered privacy to move and meet without being seen, yet it also stripped away cover. Every sound carried, every vehicle stood out, and there was no crowd to disappear into. On a slow, quiet night, whoever was better prepared gained the advantage, and whoever made a mistake had nowhere to hide.

"Why do you think they left so abruptly?" Mike said, breaking the silence.

"I don't know for sure. Maybe he really did have something to do," Sam replied.

"He did have a deer in the headlights look when you asked about his company. We know he doesn't have one," Mike said.

"Why would she tell me he has one then?" Sam asked.

Mike looked at Sam. "You two had just met. Do you think she was going to say her boyfriend is a drug dealer and the leader of a motorcycle gang? It was a quick, easy way to explain the truth away."

Sam nodded. "I don't think she told him."

"The way the night unfolded didn't work well for her. She was more of an arm piece instead of a girlfriend. And that creepy smile of his, I've found that there is always something worse behind the smile."

As they crossed 9th Street, the quiet night was broken by the rumble of diesel engines firing up. Once they got closer, they could see the old baseball field next to the old Unified School building. Three trucks sat backed in close under portable light towers, their diesel engines idling low.

A lowboy trailer was being stripped first, chains clinking as a crane lifted a slab of steel that rose slowly enough to make everyone stop and watch. Forklifts waited, then moved in, backing up with sharp beeps as soon as a crate touched the ground. A dozen men worked silently, in hard hats, gloves, and reflective vests. One who looked like a supervisor stood off to the side, clipboard in hand.

Long, wrapped cylinders and awkward ducting vanished through the rear service doors. Two men who weren't dressed like labor stood apart near the fence, watching the street more than the work. The whole operation was calm, methodical, and expensive looking.

Sam and Mike paused to watch.

"What do you make of that?" Sam asked.

"It's a little late for deliveries," Mike commented.

"Maybe it's too hot to work during the day," Sam said.

"I think we have been doing this too long, when we suspect everything," Mike said.

Sam looked at Mike. "Yes, but sometimes the little things turn out to be the thing we are looking for."

Sam started walking again. Mike stayed a little longer before turning and catching up with Sam.

Across town, on North 7th Street near the elementary school, Johnny slammed the front door closed to the Airbnb.

"What the hell was that?" Johnny screamed at Lucia.

"What are you talking about?" Lucia tried to remain calm as she retreated into the kitchen.

"That crap about the re-creation stuff. You made me look stupid," Johnny yelled.

"I didn't have time to tell you. She asked what you did for a living. It just came out," Lucia said as she backed into the kitchen island.

Johnny moved forward menacingly, glaring at her.

"You like him?" Johnny growled.

Lucia gave Johnny a puzzled look. "Who, him?"

Lucia yelped as he grabbed her arm and pulled her closer.

"You're hurting me," Lucia cried.

Johnny raised his hand.

"You embarrassed me. Here's your receipt."

Lucia heard a flat crack followed by a flash of pain. Then the taste of iron from the blood of her shattered lip as Johnny hit her with the back of his hand. With his other hand, he shoved her against the counter. She felt a flash of pain as her ribs hit the edge. She crumbled to the floor. Lucia thought that if she pretended to be passed out, he would stop his assault. She heard footsteps walking away and then the slam of the front door, soon followed by the muffled noise of a motorcycle starting and driving away.

Tears came to her eyes from the pain as she tried to stand. Instead, she crawled to the couch in the living room on all fours. The pain in her ribs was almost unbearable. Every breath hurt. Lucia made it onto the couch. She curled up into a fetal position and cried herself to sleep.

CHAPTER 15

The following morning, just after sunrise, six hundred miles north of Tombstone, Jerry rode into Moab, Utah. The sun-bleached roadway cut through the town at the edge of red rock country. The road was clean and nearly empty of traffic, marked with bike-lane symbols and long white lines that stretched toward the horizon. To Jerry's left, a low, rust-colored hillside rose sharply from the shoulder, bare except for scrub and loose stone, with a lone billboard advertising the Moab Museum. To his right, he passed sidewalks, small trees, power poles, and low buildings on the outskirts of town. The sky was cloudless, pale blue. Jerry breathed in the cool, fresh morning air.

Jerry found Red Mesa Graphics & Trophy. The place was exactly where Johnny had said it would be. Two blocks off Main, tucked between a Jeep rental place and a shuttered souvenir shop selling sun-bleached dreamcatchers.

Jerry parked his bike, dismounted, and looked up at the sun-faded sign as he walked up to a window.

Jerry put his hand to his forehead and looked inside through the dusty glass. He saw cases holding bowling trophies and off-road race plaques. The lights were on, and he saw an old, gray-haired man wearing wire-frame glasses standing behind the counter. Jerry tapped on the glass. The man looked up and took his time coming to the door.

There was a jingling of keys and the click of the lock turning. The door opened just enough to see the man's face and half his body. His face was lean and weathered, darkened and creased by a lifetime of desert sun and wind. Deep lines framed his eyes and mouth. The wire-rim glasses sat crooked on his once broken nose. His light blue-gray eyes sat back under heavy brows. The man kept his thinning hair short. He wore a faded work shirt with the sleeves rolled up, heavy denim pants, and scuffed leather boots. In the man's left ear was a small silver earring.

"Good morning," the man said. His voice sounded strong.

"I'm here to pick up something," Jerry said.

"Lots of people come here to pick up something," the man said.

"Johnny sent me and told me to ask for Eli," Jerry said.

"I'm Eli. You got something for me?" Eli asked.

"You mind if we do this inside?" Jerry asked.

"Yeah, the other guy said there would be somebody else to do the pickup," Eli said.

That sounded odd to Jerry, but he didn't know why.

He pushed the door open to let Jerry in. Once inside, Eli locked the door and walked back to the counter.

Inside smelled like dust, metal, and old carpet cleaner. Blank, dust-covered bowling trophies, plaques, and participation medals lined the walls.

"You're early," Eli said.

"I like to get things done before the day gets too hot. I've got a long ride ahead of me," Jerry said.

"You here for the plates?" Eli asked.

"Yes," Jerry said.

"You got the money?" Eli asked.

"Let's see the plates, and then you see the cash," Jerry said.

Eli laughed and gestured toward the back. "This isn't some kind of illegal transaction."

Jerry followed Eli past the old printing press. The place looked a little like a shrine to printers. "What is this place?" Jerry asked.

"I bought the place from a guy who thought he was going to corner the market on printing in the Moab area. Like everyone with a dream that comes out here, he didn't think it all the way through," Eli said as he pointed to a picture on the wall.

An old photo hung on one wall of an old man with rectangular glasses, long gray hair, and a full gray beard, his face marked by age lines. The words "Keith Our Founder" were written on a small, rusted plaque affixed to the bottom.

Eli led Jerry into a brightly lit machine shop. A black Pelican box sat on a workbench. Eli opened it with a smile. The hard case was lined with dark foam. Four rectangular metal printing plates were neatly fitted into custom-cut slots, each engraved with detailed currency-style designs. At the bottom of the case were white cotton gloves.

The engravings looked strange to Jerry. He moved closer to examine the plates' details. Jerry's heart began to beat faster as he read the words. The Confederate States of America was engraved on one of the plates. He looked over the plates, which were in different denominations. One in particular caught his attention.

At the center of the note was a finely engraved vignette of a classical building, rendered in delicate lines that draw the eye across the bill. On the right, an oval portrait of a stern-looking man was deeply engraved, with tight cross-hatching that added shadow and dimension. The denomination "5" appeared prominently in several places, and a signature was engraved in the lower-right corner.

Jerry instinctively reached into his pocket and fingered the burnt paper inside it. He started to pull it out and then stopped. He would have to wait to compare the plate and the bill. Now he had to get out of here.

"What do you think?" Eli asked with a proud smile.

"They're beautiful," Jerry said.

He reached inside his jacket, pulled out the money, and set it on the workbench. Eli counted it, satisfied, then put it in his front pocket. He reached under the bench, pulled out a second case, and opened it to show Jerry another set of plates. He closed both cases and handed them to Jerry.

"Is this what you do for a living?" Jerry asked.

"Look around this shop," Eli gestured. "I'm a tool-and-die maker. I can cut industrial stamping plates for part numbers, serials, and inspection marks. I've made seals and embossing plates for companies that needed raised logos on paper or packaging. I've engraved nameplates and data plates for machinery, ratings, warnings, and manufacturer marks. I've also done security-style plates for certificates, permits, and tickets, where fine lines and clean impressions matter. Once you know how steel cuts and how ink behaves under pressure, money plates are no harder than any of the others. Just takes more patience and less room for mistakes. If somebody wants to pay me to make engraving plates for the Confederate States of America, I don't care as long as the money comes from the current United States."

Jerry nodded. He admired the man's skills.

"I need to get going," he said.

Eli led him out of the shop and back to the front door. He put the key in the lock and turned to Jerry.

"Oh, one other thing. Make sure you tell them to do the wash."

"What?"

"Sorry, I forgot you're not a printer. Think of washing as a cleaning step after the ink is already on the paper. After the sheets come off the press, the ink is set enough that it won't smear, but there's still excess oils from the ink, plate residue, and loose pigment on the surface. The printed sheets are lightly rinsed or wiped with a controlled solution to remove the residue.

"The wash doesn't remove the image. It only takes off what didn't bond to the paper. When it's done right, the lines look sharper, the paper feels cleaner, and the ink will dry more evenly. After washing, the sheets go straight to drying."

"Thanks for the explanation. I'll make sure to remind them," Jerry said.

Eli opened the door and watched Jerry load the cases in his saddlebags. Jerry put on his helmet, started the bike, looked back, and waved goodbye. Eli heard Jerry ride away as he closed and locked the door.

Jerry made his way out of town riding south on US 191. He stopped to fill up and grabbed a few water bottles for the trip. He checked his route on his phone.

Once he crossed the state line into Arizona, he would follow it until it intersected U.S. 160, then turn right toward Kayenta and continue south until it ended at U.S. 89. After following that highway to Flagstaff, he would pick up I-17. That would lead him to I-10 into Benson, and finally to Historic U.S. 80, which led to Tombstone.

He sighed. There was at least a ten-hour ride ahead of him, and he was already tired from the morning's ride. He knew he would have to stop to sleep. Jerry realized he would never find out how Mark died if he didn't make it. This whole thing would be for nothing.

He dialed a number on his phone that Johnny had given him.

"Hello," a male voice said.

Jerry didn't recognize the voice.

"I've got your package, but it will be tomorrow before I get there," Jerry said.

"No problem, amigo," the voice said.

The line went dead. Jerry gave his phone a strange look. There was a message that read: "Call completed." Jerry shrugged and put it back in his pocket as he mounted his motorcycle and started the journey.

An hour later, in Tombstone, Royce parked the light blue GTO convertible, with the top down, in front of the old Unified School building. The school was on Old Historic Highway 80, also called Fremont Street. Colt rested an arm on the door as he sat in the passenger seat. The building sat on the corner of Fremont and Sixth Street, with Allen Street running behind it.

The two men wore blade sunglasses, light-colored polo shirts, and casual slacks. They stood out against the white leather interior. The pair looked like two middle-aged businessmen instead of members of a motorcycle club.

Royce put the car in park, turned off the motor, and looked over at Colt.

"Well, friend, let's go see your new business," Royce said.

The men got out of the car and started up the front walk to the front doors. Dry grass filled the front yard, giving the place a worn, deserted feel. Colt looked at the two-story, light-colored stucco building, which appeared tired and run-down.

It had once been a school, now just another reminder of a different time. The windows and the bottom floors were boarded up. The wood was weathered and uneven in color. This matched the front doors, which were boarded over with plywood cut to fit the doorway and fastened directly across the opening.

Two tall palm trees flanked the walk. What got Colt's attention was that one was bald, and the other had green palm leaves.

Colt looked at Royce. "How much?"

"For the place? I got it for about half a million. I convinced the agent I was going to use some of the proceeds from the printing shop to help the community," Royce said.

Colt patted Royce on the back. "Good job. Maybe I will just do that. The more legitimate things we do, the less heat we take."

Royce stopped at the door.

"Two coming in!" he yelled.

Royce opened the front door, and the two men walked inside. There was one of Colt's men sitting with a shotgun. The man waved as he watched Colt and Royce walk by. The two men put their sunglasses on the tops of their heads.

The whir of power drills and hammers could be heard.

"There's plenty of space for the vaults. The printing is set up in the old gym, and we can load and unload without prying eyes on the side near the old ball field," Royce said.

"Great, but it's a little warm in here. What about the air conditioning?" Colt asked.

"It will be a week before we can get anyone to come out," Royce said.

"I guess we will have to print at night for a while," Colt said.

They made their way through the building to the gym.

Colt looked at the long steel press sitting where the basketball court used to be, bolted to the floor, its frame dull gray and streaked with oil. Rollers, ink housings, and exposed gears lined the sides, with thick cables and hoses running to power units along the wall. Large rolls of paper were ready to be threaded through the press to be transformed into flat, freshly printed sheets. Then those sheets were stacked on pallets. Portable lights hung from stands to compensate for the gym's lighting, and the air smelled of ink and solvent.

"Wow," Colt said.

"The locker rooms have been converted into wash and drying rooms," Royce said.

"When will the new plates be here?" Colt asked.

"Ringo says one more day," Royce answered.

"Good. I will finally be rid of Ringo for good," Colt said.

Royce smiled. "Finally."

"Have you heard from Mango? He went to make the route payment a couple of days ago. I've called his phone. I just got a busy signal."

"I'm sure he's fine," Royce said.

"When can we start printing?" Colt asked.

"We could start tonight if we had the plates," Royce said.

"Use the old plates and do a few runs to get the machine warmed up," Colt said.

"I'll get it started after the sun goes down. It should be a little cooler," Royce said.

The two headed back out to the car.

CHAPTER 16

Two blocks away, Sam walked into the Spur Western Wear store on Allen Street.

Sam paused just inside the doorway and let her eyes adjust. The shop was bigger than it looked from the outside, with high ceilings, exposed beams, and warm lights hanging over rows of clothing and mannequins standing on wooden bases, one dressed in a faded blue suit jacket over a patterned shirt, another in a long, dusty-rose dress.

"Can I help you?" a young woman asked.

Sam turned to the voice. The woman was behind the counter.

"Hi, I'm looking for a white blouse my friend had on yesterday. She said she bought it here," Sam said.

The woman's face lit up, "Really. What's her name?"

"Lucy," Sam said.

"Yes, she is a regular. She can wear almost anything. I wish I had her figure," the woman said.

Sam nodded in agreement. The phone rang.

"Excuse me," the woman said as she answered the phone.

Sam could only hear one side of the conversation.

"Hello, Hi Lucy, Yes, I can have it delivered. Leave it at the door. Let me get the address."

The woman wrote something down on a piece of paper.

"I hope you get better," the woman said and hung up the phone.

She came around the counter. "Will you excuse me for a moment. I need to fill this delivery order."

"Take your time," Sam said.

While the woman went to a back room. Sam wandered over to the counter to look at some jewelry. She saw the pad. Two long-sleeved shirts, two silk scarves, and a pair of flats. The other thing she saw was the address on 7th Street.

Sam repeated the address in her head enough times until she was sure she would remember it.

Sam heard footsteps and turned to see the woman coming from the back.

"Thank you for waiting," the woman said.

"I'm looking for a white sleeveless French-style blouse," Sam said.

"I have one right here. You look like a size 3. It might be a little tight, but you can always exchange it," the woman said as she walked to a shelf across the room.

She found it and returned to the counter. "Will there be anything else?"

"No, I think that's it," Sam said as she paid.

The woman handed Sam the bag with the blouse. Sam turned and walked out. She turned right to head back to the RV park.

Sam's thought as she walked down the wooden-planked sidewalk, *That's pretty strange. Lucy seemed fine when she left last night. Why the delivery? Maybe that's how she had all her things delivered. She was a kept woman after all. But why the long sleeves and scarves? It bothers me, but I can't explain why.*

Sam made it back to the RV. The rest of the team was already inside. Just before she stepped inside, she heard the shots from the re-creation of the shootout at O.K. Corral that was only a block away. She opened the door, and felt the rush of cool air from inside. The team was seated at the main table. This would be the daily situational briefing. Sam took a seat at the table.

"Good morning, everyone," Sam said.

"Good morning," the group said in unison.

"What is the situation today?" Sam asked.

Greg spoke first. "Jerry has made his pickup in Moab and is en route here. He likely won't make it here today, but it is a possibility."

"Then we need to make sure we are ready for him to arrive today," Sam said.

"He's been pretty tight-lipped," Greg said.

"Alex, can you give me an assessment of Jerry's mindset?"

"I haven't interviewed Jerry directly, so this is provisional. Based on reports, he's showing signs of acute stress after his friend's death. No indication of cognitive impairment or disorganized thinking. His actions appear goal-directed and consistent with a focused investigative response rather than impulsivity."

She paused. "Risk tolerance is elevated, but there's no evidence of panic, dissociation, or emotional collapse. He's functioning, oriented, and operational. That said, this level of sustained drive usually delays processing. When the immediate objective ends, the psychological impact is likely to surface."

"Like what types of psychological impact?" Sam asked.

"Most likely outcomes are delayed grief and post-event stress reactions," she said.

"That can include intrusive memories of the scene, sleep disruption, hypervigilance, irritability, and impaired judgment once the immediate threat or objective is removed. In agents like Jerry, it often presents as emotional flattening first, followed by a rebound once the mission pressure drops.

"If it goes untreated," she added, "you're looking at classic post-traumatic stress patterns rather than a breakdown in the field."

"How do we deal with him when he gets here?" Greg asked.

"Don't confront him, don't slow him down, and don't try to process it with him yet," she said. "Right now, his focus is what's keeping him functional. Interfering with that increases the risk of bad decisions."

She continued, "Keep instructions clear and task-based. Limit variables, no surprises. Pair him with someone steady, not emotional. Once the delivery is done and he's off the bike, you pull him, give him a controlled pause, and support him with food, hydration, and sleep. That's when you assess for cracks."

She looked at Sam. "Until then, treat him as operational."

Sam looked around the table. "I know we all care about Jerry, but we still have to figure out how all of this fits together. His friend Mark may have been murdered. What I don't want is for this to turn into a Wyatt Earp vendetta. I know the metaphor isn't lost on any of you, given our current location.

"Garrett, what do you have for me?" Sam asked.

"We've got plenty of firepower if we need it. The SUV and the RV have PMCS'd and are ready."

Sam turned to Greg. "Greg, what do you have?"

"I've been tracking Jerry. He has been making his regular check-ins. His last location was outside of Tuba City, Arizona." Greg checked his watch. "He should check in, in another hour."

"Why did you say he probably wouldn't make it until tomorrow?" Sam asked.

"It's roughly a ten-hour nonstop ride from Moab to Tombstone. He will have to make at least three stops for gas. Then factor in weather, terrain, and the regular stress of riding. Even with minimal stops, that will add an hour. It's a long ride. I'm going to encourage him to take an overnight stop."

"I agree with Greg. He should take a break," Alex added.

"It would give us a little bit more time to figure out what is going on," Mike said.

Everyone nodded in agreement. Sam looked at Mike.

"Okay, what do you have?"

"Tombstone isn't an open motorcycle club town. Nobody claims it. Too small, too many tourists, too much law enforcement. Any gang activity here stays temporary and quiet.

"Outsiders don't roll in packs. No colors downtown. No loitering. Anyone smart moves in ones or twos and blends in."

He leaned forward. "Rule is business first, ego second. Nobody disrupts the tourist money. Anyone who does gets pressure from law enforcement, business owners, and other players who don't want heat.

"Real business doesn't happen in town. All of that stays outside city limits. Tombstone is just the waypoint. If Jerry's riding in alone as a courier, that tracks. Low profile, low risk."

"What are the printing plates for?" Garrett asked.

Greg shrugged slightly as he spoke. "Tombstone makes sense on the surface. Tourists, reenactments, and people expect weird historical stuff, so printing old Confederate bills wouldn't draw much attention. Beyond that, I can only guess. It could be symbolism, could be an internal thing, or maybe they're just testing a process somewhere quiet. Point is, it's a good place to hide something you don't want looked at too closely."

"All right. We'll keep an eye on the old school building. Let's go out and act like we are making a movie," Sam said.

Mike got up and closed the door as he went into the back of the RV. Garrett stood up, put his ball cap on, and headed outside.

"I'm going to wait until Jerry checks in before I venture out," Greg said.

Sam nodded. She motioned to her sister to follow her outside.

Alex got up and followed. Once outside, Sam turned to Alex.

"I need to run something by you."

The two women walked over to a picnic table under a tree and sat down.

"Maybe it's nothing," Sam said.

Alex listened, arms folded, as Sam explained what had happened in the shop.

Alex didn't answer right away. She looked away as she thought. Once that was done, she turned and looked at Sam.

"I saw them together," she said. "She changed around him. Pulled in, watched him more than the room. That usually means someone's careful, not comfortable.

"Long sleeves, scarves, having them delivered, those aren't strange by themselves. Together, they tell me she's managing how she's seen and when she's seen. I don't know what's going on with her. But I don't think she's fine, and I don't think the boyfriend's harmless."

"I've got the address memorized. Let's take a look after dark," Sam said.

Just as Sam had finished, Mike stepped out of the RV, dressed like an 1800's cowboy with six-guns and all.

Sam turned to see Mike. "Where are you going, cowboy?"

"I thought while I'm in Tombstone, I'd dress for the part. I'm going to just walk around and see what I see," Mike said.

"You might be mistaken for a reenactor," Alex said.

Mike tipped his hat and smiled. "I can only hope."

They watched as Mike walked off, the sound of gravel crunching under his boots.

Alex turned back to Sam, who was still watching Mike.

"I think he still has feelings for you, and you for him," Alex whispered.

Sam snapped her head to look at Alex. "Don't be silly."

"I'm your sister. I can see it," Alex pushed.

Sam stood up. "There's no time for that. We have a mission to complete."

Alex watched her sister storm off the RV.

Once inside, Greg looked up at Sam. "I just heard from Jerry. He's stopping for the night outside of Munds, Arizona. He's renting a cabin for the night. He said the road from Moab across northern Arizona was a rough ride and a nightmare for his body."

"Good. When does he get here tomorrow?"

"Just before sundown, if there aren't any other delays," Greg said.

"Keep me informed of any changes, please," Sam said.

"Yes, ma'am," Greg replied, smiling.

"I'm going for a walk around town. You should have some time to get some sleep. I know you've been burning the midnight oil to keep up with communications."

"I'm waiting for Mark's autopsy report to come in. I expect it in the next few hours.

"All right. I'm going out," Sam said and left.

The day passed uneventfully and Garrett was making dinner for the team. The team rotated making dinner on missions like this, which gave them time to relax and talk together. Garrett made the same thing every time. Spaghetti, it was always spaghetti.

He placed the pot of pasta in the middle of the table and the sauce to the side. Everyone took turns serving themselves.

"Why spaghetti?" Greg asked.

"Mike knows why," Garrett said, continuing. "Spaghetti is cheap, fills you up, and gives you carbs that last. You can make a lot of it fast. It doesn't go bad. You don't have to think about it. If you burn a day doing hard work, it replaces what you used."

"He's right," Alex said.

Everyone began to eat.

"It sounds like everyone in town is excited by the new printing company that's set up shop in the old Unified School building," Garrett said.

"In a small town that depends on tourism, new money is good money," Mike added.

"The autopsy report came in on Mark," Greg said.

"What were the results?" Sam asked.

"I haven't read it. I was going to have Alex review it," Greg said.

"What does everyone have planned for tonight?" Sam asked.

"I'm going to the VFW across the street with Mike. I was told that's where a lot of locals hang out," Garrett said.

"I'm staying here," Greg said.

Everyone looked down, and no one spoke for a moment.

Sam broke the silence. "Alex and I are going to take the SUV and check out an address that may be Ringo's. Nothing risky, just a little drive around."

After dinner, Mike and Garrett had left, Alex was outside in the SUV and Sam was about to leave. She stopped and turned to Greg.

"Hey, Greg. I appreciate what you're doing, monitoring the communications and keeping tabs on Jerry. You and he are close; we are all worried about Jerry, but don't let it become an obsession for you. He's going to need all the help he can get when he gets here."

Greg nodded. "Thanks, Sam. You might be right. I'm internalizing things too much."

"That's all. See you in a few hours," Sam said as she left.

Sam climbed into the SUV, and Alex drove out of the RV site.

"The address is off 7th Street near the elementary school," she said.

"We'll drive around in the neighborhoods for a while. Hopefully, we won't look too obvious," Alex said.

"Let's hope all of us out and about will make people think we are just looking for night shooting locations," Sam added.

Over at the old Unified School, Royce had just come out of the locker rooms. Scott Miller, a twenty-five-year-old college dropout who had come to Tombstone one summer and stayed when his car had broken down, stood by the end of the printer. He was wearing a white bio-hazard suit with tennis shoes. He held a full-face respirator and blue rubber gloves.

Royce came up to him. "All you have to do is take the sheets, put them on the racks, put them in the showers, and move them into the drying room."

Scott nodded his head. "I think I can do that."

"Good. I'll be back to check on you in a few hours," Royce said.

"Can I take breaks?" Scott asked.

"Sure, just make sure the machine doesn't get backed up. If you smoke, do it outside by the old baseball field. I don't think fire and these chemicals will mix too well," Royce said.

Royce waved Scott over to the printing machine and explained how to turn it on and off. Then, Royce had Scott explain it to him. Satisfied, Royce watched as Scott started the process. He watched one run of the paper and left.

Alex and Sam drove slowly through the neighborhoods before turning on 7th Street.

"The place should be by itself on the left," Sam said.

"I think I see it off in the distance," Alex said.

"Looks like nobody is home. No lights on and nothing in the driveway," Sam said.

"You're sure that was the right address?" Alex said.

"I'm positive," Sam said.

"Maybe they moved," Alex speculated.

They kept the speed limit as they drove past and turned left on North Street. After a few minutes, Alex realized she had gone the wrong way.

"I made a wrong turn. This will lead us into a dead end if the map is correct. I've got to turn around," Alex said, turning the SUV around.

They started back up 7th Street and saw a motorcycle coming in the opposite direction. It slowed and turned into the driveway of the house they had passed. Alex pulled her hat down, and Sam ducked down as they passed. Alex looked in her rear-view mirror as she casually turned away up East Stafford Street.

"It's safe," Alex said.

Sam popped back up.

"Single rider, male, no sign of your friend," Alex said.

Sam looked out the window as she thought. Was Lucia still there? Was she dead?

While Sam thought about Lucia, Scott Miller figured out how much time he had for a smoke break and headed outside. He pulled off his respirator. The warm night air felt cool against his sweat-stained face. He took off his gloves and stuffed them into one of the outer cargo pockets. His suit had some wet spots from the paper wash. His fingers brushed against them as he unzipped his suit to get his pack of cigarettes. He fished out a cigarette, and it fell to the ground.

"Crap," he murmured as he bent down to pick it up.

A drop of the wash splashed on the cigarette when he picked it up.

He rolled his eyes and looked at it.

No big deal. It'll dry from the heat as I smoke it, he thought.

He pulled out his lighter and lit his cigarette.

He took a long drag and held it for a moment. He did a long exhale, and the plume of smoke disappeared into the night sky. Then he took another draw. He felt sudden euphoria followed by a bout of dizziness, like when your blood pressure suddenly drops. He stumbled for a moment and then began to walk, half stumbling, toward Allen Street. The cigarette was still between his fingers. Scott saw that the streetlights had a weird halo around them, and then the ground rushed up and nothing.

Alex turned left onto 2nd Street towards Fremont. Once there, she turned left and drove past the old school. She then turned right onto South 9th Street, then right onto East Allen Street.

Sam was the first to see it.

"What's that white thing near the road?" Sam pointed.

Alex looked where Sam had pointed and knew instantly what it was. A body. Alex pulled up and stopped near Scott with her headlights illuminating his body.

"Call 911," Alex said as she slammed the SUV into park and ran to the back to get her medical bag.

Scott lay face down near the curb, one arm bent under him, the other stretched out as if he'd tried to catch himself. Alex slipped on a mask and surgical gloves before touching him.

When she rolled him onto his back, the hood of the suit fell away from his face. His skin was pale, his lips tinged faintly blue, and his eyes half-lidded. She knew he was dead but felt for a pulse anyway. She didn't find any. His body was still warm. Whatever killed him did it quickly. She noticed the front of the suit was slightly damp and wrinkled. She touched the damp area and held it up to the light. It glistened in the headlight.

Sam ran up to help. Alex held up her hand.

"Stay back, I don't know what I got here." Alex's voice was muffled.

Sirens blared from somewhere. EMS and the Fire Department arrived a few minutes later.

A paramedic climbed out of the passenger side of the ambulance, grabbed gear from a side compartment, and rushed over to Alex.

He put on his mask and surgical gloves. "What do we have?"

"We found him this way. I checked his pulse and got nothing," Alex said.

The paramedic checked for a pulse and waved to his partner. He pulled out the gurney from the back of the ambulance. There was radio chatter, and the fire truck drove off. A police patrol car pulled up, and an officer got out and walked over as the paramedics were loading Scott's lifeless body, now covered by a sheet, into the ambulance.

Alex picked up her PPE, put it into a biohazard bag, and sealed it

"Good evening, ladies. I'll need to make a report," the officer said.

They relayed how they had come across the body and the cover story of what they were doing in Tombstone. The officer didn't ask any more questions.

"Does this happen a lot?" Alex asked.

"More than I would like to admit. The people of this town are great, but drugs have found their way even to Tombstone," the officer said.

"What about what he was wearing?" Sam asked.

"I don't know. I'll have one of the detectives figure it out. I've got a disturbance call to answer." He got back in his patrol car and drove off.

Alex waited a moment to make sure the officer wasn't going to turn around. She looked at the old school building and the path the dead man would likely have taken, pulled out a flashlight, and walked slowly toward the building. She found the half-burned cigarette. She went back to her kit and, using a pair of tweezers, put it into a sealed biohazard bag.

She got back inside the SUV and started it.

"What was that all about?" Sam asked.

"I don't know. Maybe something, maybe nothing. There weren't any marks on the guy's body. So, my hunch is it was something he ingested," Alex explained.

"Maybe it was pills," Sam said.

"Let's get back to the RV. I need a shower after touching a dead body," Alex said.

An hour later, Royce came back to the printing operation to find it had jammed and shut down. He looked around for Scott and didn't find him.

CHAPTER 17

Jerry woke up to a knock on the door. He checked the time. It was 10 o'clock in the morning. He swung his feet out of bed and went to the door.

"Yes," he said without opening the door.

"Just a reminder, checkout is at eleven," a muffled female voice said.

"Thank you," Jerry said.

He quickly showered, dressed, and headed out the door. He had seven hours before he would reach Tombstone.

Alex was sitting outside at the picnic table, reading Mark's autopsy report on a tablet.

Alex read the report again, then went back and read the opinion again. She had read it three times.

Cause of death: acute drug toxicity.

The toxicology section listed heroin and ketamine, both present, but neither at a level that should have killed a healthy adult. She paused. That combination alone didn't explain its speed. It didn't explain collapsing in the open air.

Lower on the page, the examiner's language changed. *Novel synthetic compound.* Unclassified. Lethal concentration. Potentiating effect. The phrasing was careful, almost restrained, as if the pathologist didn't want to speculate.

Alex's eyes went back to a single line in the opinion: Death resulted from acute toxicity due to a novel synthetic drug, with heroin and ketamine acting as contributing factors. The absence of injection sites and the chemical properties of the synthetic compound suggest non-injection exposure, possibly transdermal or incidental contact.

The absence of injection sites suggests non-injection exposure.

She read that sentence three times.

Non-injection. Incidental contact. Dermal absorption.

Alex leaned back and set the tablet down. She looked up at nothing and thought about the residue on the gloves she'd sealed away. The way it had glistened. The way it hadn't smelled. She continued to let her thoughts flow.

Whatever killed Mark was quick. If this were through dermal absorption, it could easily be made into an aerosol and used on a crowd or an individual. But wait, she hadn't been affected.

Did Mark stumble onto a WMD? If so, then what about the guy last night? Had somebody created a bioweapon and been experimenting on people on the fringes of society? The only way to know was to dig deeper.

Greg came out of the RV and walked over to Alex.

"Jerry just checked in. He woke up late. He should be here just after sundown."

"Good to know," Alex said as she stood up and headed to the RV.

Greg followed her inside.

"Where are Garrett and Mike?" Alex asked.

"At the O.K. Corral reenactment," Sam said.

"Good, now I need both of you to wait outside while I do a lab test," Alex said without thinking.

Sam gave her sister a puzzled look. "What?"

"I just read Mark's autopsy report. I think the guy last night and Mark's death have a common denominator, but I have to do a test in a controlled environment. Which means I need you two to wait outside, because if I'm wrong, I'll need an EpiPen and EMS," Alex explained, like giving a drink order.

Alarm replaced Sam's surprised look.

"I should be all right," Alex said as he grabbed the SUV keys and left the RV.

Greg and Sam followed her out.

"Slow down. I'm not understanding," Sam said.

Alex turned abruptly. "Trust me. I'll explain it in a moment. Give me ten minutes."

She grabbed he medical kit from the SUV and disappeared into the RV. The only sound was the click of the lock.

Greg and Alex looked at each other with puzzled expressions. As they waited, they heard the lavatory exhaust fan turn on. After a few moments, they were reminded by the heat they were standing in direct sunlight. They moved under a tree and waited.

"What do we do if she doesn't come out?" Sam asked.

"I've got another set of keys. We'll wait ten minutes, then knock, and if we don't get an answer, then go in," Greg said, checking his watch.

The minutes dragged on, then the door flew open, and Alex came running out.

"Eureka!" Alex yelled.

"You want to let the rest in on your discovery?" Sam said, relieved.

Alex waved them back to the RV. "Let's get out of the heat."

Greg and Sam followed her back inside and sat down.

"I looked at Mark's report and saw that whatever killed him caused pulmonary edema, which meant it had to be respiratory. The guy last night had no visible injection marks that I could tell. The other thing, if he was shooting up, he wouldn't have put his suit back on. Could have been pills, but I checked the substance on my gloves and found the same markers as were listed in the report. I then tested the half-smoked cigarette. The same synthetic markers were also on paper all the way to the burnt end. Ergo, the synthetic wasn't poisonous by itself. It only became dangerous after the heat changed it. Same substance, different chemistry," Alex explained.

"That's a lot to base on a field test," Greg said.

"I know, but it's the best I have for right now. If I can get last night's autopsy, then I could have more to go on," Alex said.

"How did two guys get exposed to the same thing a thousand miles apart?" Sam asked.

"I don't know, but I bet it's got something to do with our new printers in town," Alex said. "I need to get inside the school and check," she added.

"Not a chance in the daytime. I don't like the nighttime either. Too many variables," Sam said.

"What do we do now?" Greg asked.

"Wait until Jerry gets here," Sam said.

At the old school, Royce watched a portly technician in overalls as he climbed down from the top of the printer.

"Well?" Royce asked, annoyed.

The technician wiped sweat from his brow with his sleeve. "A three maybe, four-day repair. The paper is jammed pretty hard, and the feeder belt will need to be replaced, then there is the cleanup of the ink sprayer," the man said.

"What if you work on it around the clock?" Royce asked.

He screwed up his mouth as he thought. "I guess I can get some guys down here from Benson. We could probably have it up and running by late tomorrow or early the next day. It would cost you a lot," the man said.

"I don't care what it costs, just get it running," Royce growled.

The man put his hands up defensively. "Hey, mister. I'm telling the truth. I'll get the guys and the belt down here right away," he said.

"Just get it running," Royce said.

Royce turned and walked away. His footsteps echoed across the wooden gymnasium floor.

One hundred and eighty miles north, Jerry was riding through Phoenix. He would be in Tombstone in three hours. After he pulled off the road and gassed up, he called Greg. Then he was back on the road to Tombstone.

The team gathered in the RV.

"We've got about three hours before Jerry gets here," Greg said.

"Alex, I will let you talk to him when he gets here," Sam said.

Mike stood up. "I think we need to eat early and do pre-combat checks, just in case."

"Agreed, we need to be prepared. I think it's your turn to cook," Sam said.

"Why yes, it is. I'll get started," Mike said and went to the kitchen.

Garrett and Greg stood up and went outside.

"I need to check my medical kit," Alex said and left.

Sam turned to Mike, who was cutting some meat. "I've talked to Alex. What do you think his mindset will be when he gets here?"

Mike picked up a meat tenderizer hammer and started to pound it against the pieces he had just cut. He stopped and placed it aside.

"His friend is dead, and he doesn't know why. He has spent the last few days trying to find out. If it were me, I would want at least my pound of flesh," Mike said.

"Vengeance then?" she asked.

"In his mind, it may be justice for his friend. Remember, we are in Tombstone. Perceptions and the truth can be different," Mike said.

"Go on," Sam said.

"Let's look at the town we are in. The gunfight commonly known as the Shootout at the O.K. Corral occurred on October 26, 1881, in a narrow vacant lot off Fremont Street in Tombstone, adjacent to the rear entrance of the O.K. Corral, rather than inside the corral itself," Mike said.

"Most people know that," Sam said.

"What you may not know is that it was once called the incident on Fremont Street, but over time, it has come to be known as what it is. Now let's look at the people involved," Mike explained.

"What does this have to do with Jerry?" Sam asked.

"To the Clantons, the Earps weren't lawmen. They were bullies wearing badges. From their perspective, the shootout at the O.K. Corral wasn't justice. It was an ambush disguised as law enforcement.

"Afterward, the Clantons saw themselves as targets. Ike Clanton viewed the Earps as men who would never stop until every Clanton ally was either dead or driven out. In their eyes, the feud was no longer about cattle rustling or threats. It was about survival.

"Wyatt Earp didn't see the Vendetta Ride as revenge. He saw it as unfinished law enforcement. After his brother Virgil was maimed and his other brother Morgan was murdered, Wyatt believed the legal system had failed completely. Courts released suspects, witnesses vanished, and justice stalled. To Wyatt, riding out with a badge and a gun was the only thing the killers understood.

"In his mind, the Vendetta Ride was about restoring order through force. He believed he was removing men who would never face trial and who would keep killing if left alone. Wyatt later framed it not as anger, but as duty carried to its grim conclusion," Mike explained.

"I understand, I don't have a problem if we have to use lethal force, if necessary, but I cannot allow Jerry to become a vigilante," Sam said.

"I agree, but Jerry may have other plans," Mike said.

"Then we have to work hard to convince him otherwise," Sam said.

Mike nodded and went back to making dinner.

CHAPTER 18

An hour after sundown, Jerry pulled up next to the RV and cut the engine. Greg was the first one out to greet him. The motor's ticking could be heard as Jerry took off his helmet and dismounted his bike.

"Good to see you," Greg said.

Jerry threw Greg the helmet. "Good to see you, buddy. I've got to make the delivery at the old school in an hour."

"Sam's in charge of the mission and wants you to hear what Alex has to say first," Greg said.

"Can it wait?" Jerry asked, slightly annoyed.

"I agree with her," Greg said.

Jerry looked at Greg and saw that he was serious.

"Let's get this over with," Jerry said as he walked to the RV.

Everyone was inside as Jerry came in. There were smiles all around.

"Are you hungry?" Mike asked.

Jerry shook his head. "I just don't have an appetite."

"It's good to see you're safe," Alex said.

"It's good to see everyone, but I don't have a lot of time," Jerry said.

"Take a seat first, Alex has something," Sam said.

Jerry didn't want to, but he was still a member of the team, and doing as he was told would get him out of there faster than arguing.

Alex related everything she had found from the cigarette butt and Mark's autopsy.

Jerry felt his anger rising, and it showed on his face.

"You're saying my friend was murdered?" Jerry said through gritted teeth.

There was silence for a moment before Alex answered.

"In a way, yes," Alex quietly answered.

"We need you. I need you to keep calm. Right now, you're the only one who can get inside the school without suspicion. We think the drug is coming from there," Sam said.

Jerry fought his thoughts of revenge. If he was going to kill a man, he wanted to be sure. He reached his hand into his pocket, pulled out a small plastic bag with the burnt bill in it, and threw it on the table.

"This is what Mark's cigarette was wrapped in," Jerry said.

"I'll get my test kit," Alex said and headed to the back.

"Don't we have to leave?" Greg asked.

"No, only if you're going to smoke it," Alex said.

Alex set her test kit on the table. She put on her surgical gloves, cut a small piece of the paper, and used tweezers to place it into an ampule. She drew a few drops of a clear liquid into an eyedropper, squeezed them into the ampule, and snapped the top closed. She shook it for a few seconds, then held it up for everyone to see the liquid turn dark red.

"That's your confirmation," she said, tapping the result with a gloved finger.

Jerry said nothing as he took the paper back and put it in his pocket.

"I'm going to need that," Jerry said as he stood up.

"Don't do anything stupid," Sam said.

"I'm not. You say you need a way into the school. I think I have an idea," Jerry said.

Jerry stepped outside and called Johnny Ringo.

"I want to make the delivery myself," Jerry said.

"Why?" Johnny asked.

"Doesn't concern you. I just want to see this to the end," Jerry said.

There was a pause. "I guess you can. Just make sure you bring the rest of my money," Johnny said.

"You will get your money. Then I want to get paid in full," Jerry said.

"They are for Frank Colt. Go to the side of the old school by the old baseball diamond. I'll let them know you're coming. Call me when it's done, and we'll meet," Johnny said.

"Deal," Jerry said and hung up.

Jerry opened the door to the RV. "I'm going to make the delivery."

Greg came outside. "Are you sure about this?"

"Yes, I've got to see who killed him and why for it to make any sense. If we are going to catch these guys, I'm the best lead we have," Jerry said.

"Are you armed?" Greg asked.

"No, it wouldn't matter. They will probably search me at the door," Jerry said.

Sam and the rest of the team came outside. Jerry turned to Sam.

"I've got to do this," Jerry said.

"I know," Sam said.

Jerry handed the helmet to Greg. "Hold on to this for me."

He got on his bike and started it. There was a low rumble from the engine. Jerry gave the throttle a quick turn and rode out to the street. The sound of his motorcycle faded as he drove down Fremont Street.

Jerry parked his bike on the side of the school. Light shone from the upper windows of the gymnasium. He felt the heat of the July night, like the dry heat of a towel that had been out in the sun. The night was quiet except for the occasional car passing down Fremont and the hum of air conditioner compressors turning on. There was a chopper parked off to his right. He stopped and looked at it for a minute. He remembered where he'd seen it before, back in Yellowstone.

He took the two black cases out of the saddlebags and headed to the old school's side door. Then he knocked.

The door opened a crack. A large man with a beard and a denim vest looked at Jerry.

"I'm here to deliver something to Frank Colt," Jerry said.

The door closed, and after a moment it opened again. The man waved Jerry inside. The room was dimly lit, but Jerry could make out a table and at least two other men the same size as the guy that let him through the door. Jerry wasn't surprised, he had figured there would be tight security the closer he got to the boss.

"Put the boxes on the table and hold your arms out to your side," the man said.

Jerry did as he was told. Someone else stepped out from behind and roughly frisked him.

"He's clean," the voice said.

"Do I get a cigarette after that?" Jerry smirked.

"Shut up, a-hole, and open the boxes," another voice said.

"If I refuse?" Jerry asked.

His question was answered by the clank of a shotgun being racked. Jerry thought about his situation. The room was not that big. From what he could figure, there were only four of them in the room. Himself, frisk guy, shotgun guy, and another guy off to the left of the table.

Jerry held his hands up. "Just a question."

He opened each case for a quick inspection.

"We'll take them now," another voice said.

"No," Jerry said.

"What did you say?" the frisk guy asked.

Jerry turned and took a step towards him. "I said no."

Frisk guy reacted just as Jerry had hoped, lunging toward him. Jerry grabbed the man's head and drove his nose into Jerry's forehead. Hearing the crunch, he felt the blood from the man's now broken nose. The guy screamed in pain. Jerry spun him left and let him go. The shotgun guy lost control of his weapon as the frisk guy crashed into him. Jerry grabbed the shotgun and drove the butt into the previous owner's face, knocking him unconscious. The final man behind the desk held his hands up.

"Put your gun on the table nice and slow," Jerry said.

The man reached behind his back, slowly drew a .38 snub-nose, and set it on the table.

"You broke my nose," the frisk guy said, sounding like a clown.

Jerry laughed and the other men laughed. Jerry swung the butt of the shotgun and hit the laughing man in the jaw, knocking him out. He then spun around and used the butt again to knock the frisk guy out. Jerry quickly checked each of his opponents for weapons. He was now in possession of six knives, five handguns, two of which were revolvers, and a shotgun. One was a .38 revolver, the other a .45 ACP. More than enough firepower, but too much to actually be practical. He disabled the automatics by dismantling them and keeping the springs. He put the snub-nosed in his jacket pocket and the .45 in his front waistband for a quick cross draw.

He opened the door and checked the hallway. It was dark except for some light from the gymnasium doors. He picked up the cases and the shotgun. Jerry realized he couldn't carry the shotgun and the cases. He quickly unloaded the rounds and put them in his other coat pocket, and jammed one of the automatic magazines into the shotgun breach. Hoping that it worked and that his new friends didn't have any more guns or shotgun rounds.

Jerry headed down the dark hallway. His jacket felt heavy, the cases felt heavy. Up ahead, he heard footsteps approaching. They sounded like more than one person. He ducked into an open, darkened classroom.

Jerry heard two men speak.

"I heard a noise at the delivery door. It's probably nothing," one man said.

"I'll check on Colt. Just in case," the other said.

Jerry waited a moment, then peered out of the room. He knew he didn't have much time before the guards were discovered. He slipped out to follow the man going to check on Colt. He didn't have to go far to watch the man.

Where else would Colt be but in the principal's office, Jerry thought.

A squeak echoed in the halls, then the rush of air as the air conditioner started.

Jerry watched the man enter the principal's office. The other man must have found his compatriots and was sounding the alarm. Jerry didn't have a plan, more of just instinct. He couldn't stay where he was. He knew he would definitely get caught.

He had to move and move now. He bolted to the office and rushed inside. Colt and the other man were surprised just enough for Jerry to drop the case in his right hand and cross-draw the .45. The two men were wearing their coats. Jerry noticed Colt's had the patch of "President."

Jerry backed up the door. He kicked a wooden door wedge under the door.

"Guns on the table," he demanded.

"You must be the courier," Colt said as he lay his two revolvers on the table.

"You too," Jerry said to the other man.

The man looked at Colt and nodded. The man placed an automatic on the desk.

Jerry collected the guns and put them on a couch where he stood near the door.

There was pounding on the door. Men were yelling, demanding to be let in.

"Looks like we have a bit of a conundrum," Colt said with a calm that Jerry didn't expect.

Jerry set the other case down and then waved the gun at the other man.

"You pick up these two cases and put them on the desk, and move back to that far corner," Jerry said.

The banging continued.

"I'm all right. Stop banging on the door," Colt shouted.

The banging stopped, and some muffled discussion was heard outside the door.

The man picked up the cases, set them on the desk, and retreated to the far right corner, away from Colt.

"What's your name?" Colt asked, keeping eye contact.

"Jerry," he replied, not breaking eye contact.

Colt studied Jerry for a moment. "What do you want?"

"What's it to you?" Jerry shot back.

"You are either the stupidest person I have ever met who has a death wish, or you want something else. Which is it?" Colt said.

"I'll tell you after business is completed. Open the case and confirm deliveries," Jerry said.

Colt carefully opened the cases. He nodded in approval as a smile crept across his face. He closed the cases and pushed them aside. Jerry reached into his pocket and pulled out the plastic bag with the burnt Confederate $5 bill.

"This came off my friend," Jerry said. "Same friend I found dead in the Badlands," he said evenly.

Colt opened the bag and pulled out the burnt remains. He stiffened, not defensively, but alert and recognized the bill immediately.

"You say this came off your dead friend in the Badlands?" Colt asked.

"Are you hard of hearing?" Jerry said.

"I need to check something, but it's in my desk drawer. It's a UV pen light," Colt said.

"All right, but if you come out with anything but it and your fingers and thumb, I will make sure that's the last thing you do," Jerry said.

Colt slowly pulled open the drawer, keeping eye contact with Jerry. He carefully pulled out the UV light and set it on the table.

"I need to turn it on and check something," Colt said.

Jerry nodded.

Colt inspected the bill with the light. When he saw the half-burnt watermark, his jaw tightened, and anger washed over him. He turned off the light and broke eye contact with Jerry.

"What's this have to do with me?" Colt asked.

"There's something on there. Something that is lethal if heated and inhaled. Someone gave that to my friend, and now he's dead. You're making Confederate replicas. This all leads back to you," Jerry said.

"You some kind of cop?" Colt asked.

"They don't let someone who spent time at the Folsom Hotel wear a badge," Jerry said.

"At least we have something in common," Colt quipped.

"We both know not to trust a con. The only real person you can trust is yourself," Jerry said.

Colt nodded.

Colt's voice stayed level. "If I wanted someone dead, I wouldn't poison paper."

"That part doesn't make sense to me. But, I know my friend died when he rolled a cigarette with that bill, and you just had a printer overdose last night," Jerry said.

Colt looked over at the guy in the corner. "Is that true?"

"Royce said he just left. The cops came by this morning asking questions, and Royce talked to them," the man said.

"You're right, we do have a conundrum," Jerry kept going before Colt can redirect. "You're the only one with the reach to contaminate a run and move it without question. That's why I came to you."

"I'm trying to make a legitimate business. Why would I get involved in drugs?" Colt asked.

"I don't care, but if it's not you, then someone in your organization," Jerry said.

"What proof do you have?" Colt said.

"Tell one of your boys to go to my right saddlebag and bring you the bundle wrapped in butcher paper. Tell them to put it on the ledge outside the window behind you and go away," Jerry said.

Colt looked at his man in the room. The man went to the door and yelled the instructions to the men outside. There was the sound of boots running down the hall. Jerry moved to a spot away from the window so no one could get a clear shot at him without hitting Colt. A few minutes later, the package was on the windowsill. Jerry waited a moment to make sure it wasn't a trick.

"Go ahead and get it," Jerry instructed.

Colt put the package on his desk and opened it.

"You know what this is," Jerry said. "And you know what it means."

Colt's eyes flicked to it, just once, and then back to Jerry.

"Where did you get this?" Colt said with gritted teeth.

"Yellowstone, at the Norris Geyser Basin, along with the toll payment," Jerry said.

Jerry didn't let Colt respond.

"No one gets close to your man Mango unless he lets them," Jerry continued. "No one handles his gear, his space, his business unless he trusts them. Mango was your Sergeant-at-Arms. The only two people could have gotten close to him. You and someone else. Someone he trusted put him in a position to die."

The room got quiet.

"One other thing was strange. When I pulled into the parking lot at Norris, someone on a chopper was riding out," Jerry said.

Colt was looking past Jerry now. Thinking.

"I didn't poison your friend, but I think I know who did," Colt said.

"There is one other thing. The guy who made the plates said not to forget the wash after printing," Jerry added.

"Son of a bitch," Colt exhaled slowly. "Ringo," he said. "This smells like Ringo.

"I'll give you safe passage out of here. But, I want you to stay a few minutes more," Colt requested.

"Why should I trust you?" Jerry asked.

"Because you want to find out who killed your friend," Colt said.

Jerry nodded.

Colt turned to his man and said, "Have Royce brought here now."

The man jumped up and gave the instructions through the door. Again, a shuffling of feet.

A few minutes later, there was a bang on the door. Colt looked at Jerry.

Jerry put his gun down and nodded.

"Bring him in," Colt yelled.

Royce was half-shoved, half-dragged into the room.

"What the hell is this all about?" Royce protested.

Colt pointed to Mango's cut. "Know anything about this?"

Royce didn't look directly at Colt, but at Jerry.

"You killed him!" Royce screamed.

"Nobody said he was dead." Colt's voice was cold.

Colt then picked up the burned bill.

"Seize him," Colt ordered.

Two men grabbed Royce by each arm and forced him to his knees.

"Look at it, brother. The only person I gave this to was you. No one could have gotten close to Mango other than you. You killed him. Tell me why?"

Royce hung his head in shame. Then he jerked his head up defiantly and tried to stand.

"Let me say my peace. Let the club decide my fate," Royce said.

Colt looked at Royce as if he were looking at something as insignificant as a speck of mud on his boot heel.

He stared for a beat, eyes flat, then a dry chuckle slipped out, low and humorless, as if the situation had finally revealed how ridiculous it was. Then the laugh came out deep and full-throated. It filled the room. Then, as quickly as it had come, it stopped. Colt just stared at Royce like he was looking at a fresh steak, contemplating not how it was going to be cooked, but what side dish to have with it.

That's when the pieces locked in for Colt. The timing. The dead printer. The contaminated wash. Mango's cut. The internal access that no outsider could have.

Colt looked at Jerry.

"How do you know the papers are polluted again?" Colt asked.

"I have a friend who is a doctor and pulled residue off her gloves when she found the printer's body last night, out by the street. And it matches the autopsy on my friend. Same synthetic. Same signature."

"And you're not a cop? You've sure got some smart friends," Colt said.

"Let him up. Time to speak up, Royce," Colt said.

Royce looked around at the group that now filled the small room.

"Colt was going to sell you out by going legit. He was going to make the fake money, and we would be like some bank or something. It wouldn't have worked," Royce explained.

"Then why spray the drugs on the money?" Colt asked.

"It would leave you holding the bag. The tainted money would be traced back to you, probably by an informant. You would get busted, and most of the gang would too. With you out of the picture, Johnny Ringo would swoop in and take the spoils," Jerry explained.

There were murmurs through the group. Colt held up his hand for silence. He pointed at Jerry.

"This man has safe passage so as not to be harmed," Colt said and continued.

"Jimmy, you're the new Sergeant-at-Arms for now. Pay the technicians. Tell them the printer doesn't need to be fixed for a couple of days. Then make sure they are out of the building. Then we will all meet in the gym. And put Royce on trial," Colt said.

The group made their way out the door, dragging Royce by the arms. He didn't resist. He knew his fate was sealed.

Once the room was clear, Jerry turned to Colt.

"I want Ringo," Jerry said flatly as he put the .45 revolver in his front waistband.

"I don't blame you, and I do owe you at least the first shot at him," Colt said.

"He wants a receipt that I made the delivery, and then he wants to meet," Jerry said.

A devious smile crossed Colt's face. "Let me help you out."

Colt pulled out his phone and dialed. "Packages delivered. Meet him in the same place as always," Colt said and hung up the phone.

Jerry looked at Colt. "Where am I going?"

Colt walked Jerry out to his motorcycle.

"That took some huge stones to do what you did. I could use a man like you as my vice president," Colt said.

"Thanks, but no thanks," Jerry said.

Colt pointed south.

"There's a place about two miles south of town, down South Old Brisbane Highway in an old quarry where South Smith Ranch Trail comes together. You'll see it when you come over the hill. Take Allen Street to South Old Brisbane, which turns off to the right. Watch yourself, there is a lot of loose gravel and animals at night."

"Seems pretty easy to find," Jerry said as he mounted his bike.

Colt turned back and went inside.

Jerry felt the extra weight in his pockets and emptied them on the ground. The sound of metal pinging as the contents were spilled on the ground. He pulled the .38 and dropped it on the ground.

He pulled out his phone and typed one word, "Goodbye," and hit send. He turned off the phone, then threw it into the empty field, started his motorcycle, and rode to meet Ringo.

Greg and Sam received Jerry's message at the same time.

"He's turned his phone off," Greg said.

"He must have made the delivery and is going after Ringo," Sam said.

"But where?" Greg asked.

"What did we talk about, no gang activity inside the city limits?" Sam said.

"Where do we start?" Greg said.

"I've got a pretty good idea who to ask. Get the team armed up and in the SUV in five minutes," Sam said.

Five minutes later, the team was in the SUV, and Sam was driving. She turned left onto 7th Street and headed to Lucia's address. Her tires screeched as they came to a stop in the driveway. She jumped out, ran up the walk, and pounded on the door.

"Lucy. This is Sam. We need you," Sam said.

There was silence, then the porch light came on. Sam stepped back. The door opened a crack. Sam could see Lucia's battered face from the porch light.

"Go away," she said.

"Our friend is going to meet him, and we think our friend is going to kill Johnny," Sam said.

"I hope he succeeds," Lucia said.

Sam wedged her foot in the door so Lucia couldn't close it.

"Leave me alone," Lucia said.

"Our friend's not a murderer. Please, you've got to know where they would meet out of town," Sam pleaded.

"He will kill me for telling you," Lucia said.

"Fine! I don't have time for this," Sam said, pulling her foot out of the door.

Lucia didn't close the door, but opened it a little wider.

"Do you have guns?" Lucia asked.

"Yes," Sam said.

"If I tell you. I must go with you, and I want a gun," Lucia said.

"We'll give you one on the way, but we have to go now," Sam said and turned to get back in the SUV.

A second later, Lucia was sitting in the rear passenger seat, giving directions. The growl of the motor revving up and the shifting automatically could be heard as Greg pulled up a map on the GPS.

Jerry was almost at the quarry when Sam made the turn onto South Old Bisbee Highway. She saw his taillight in the distance and cut her lights. Jerry rode over one rise and then down the second, which rose a little more than the last. Jerry rolled into the deserted quarry. Sam pulled off the road and cut the engine. The quarry would be just over the rise.

Then, farther south, Jerry heard the buzz of motorcycle engines getting louder. Their lights pierced the darkness as they flowed into the quarry. The riders circled around Jerry. Dust obscured the exact number, but he perceived there were at least ten riders.

Then the circle formed up, and the desert went quiet when the engines cut.

The headlights washed the sand and scrub in hard white beams. Johnny's men shifted, hands loose at their sides, eyes scanning the dark.

The silence was broken by the blast of a shotgun as Greg walked into the well of light. Everyone flinched.

"Let's keep this a fair fight," Greg declared, leveling the barrel at the group.

"I hope you got more than that," Johnny laughed.

Figures appeared behind the bikes. A couple of Johnny's guys flinched hard, spinning around, weapons half-raised. One of them backed up without meaning to into something solid.

Someone muttered, "Jesus—"

Garrett whispered, "I am death."

The man stood frozen.

Across the circle, Mike stood in the shadows and saw a man fingering his handgun.

"I wouldn't, fatty. It's hard to eat cheeseburgers without your fingers," Mike warned in a voice that sounded from everywhere.

A few of the bikers peeled off immediately. No argument. No bravado. Engines just roared back to life and disappeared into the darkness, dust hanging in the air behind them. Nobody stopped them.

The rest stayed put, frozen between pride and instinct.

Then Lucia stepped forward.

She moved slowly, deliberately, until the motorcycle lights caught her face.

The bruises and broken lip were impossible to miss now. Dark. Swollen.

Ugly.

She didn't raise her voice.

"Take a good look," she said. "Your leader did this to me."

Johnny exploded.

"That's a lie!" he shouted, stepping forward. "She's lying to you!"

Lucia didn't flinch.

"Oh, am I?"

She turned her head slightly, letting the light sit on the bruise.

"Does anyone here remember Larry and Jeff?" she asked. "The two prospects?"

A ripple went through the group. Eyes shifted. No one answered.

"I watched him blow them into smithereens out in the desert near Tucson," Lucia said, calm as stone. "No warning. No hesitation."

Johnny lunged a step closer. "Shut up!"

Lucia didn't even look at him.

"If he'll do that to them," she continued, "and beat me—what do you think happens to you the first time you disappoint him?"

Silence.

One of the men lowered his eyes. Another took a step back. A third looked over his shoulder, suddenly very aware of someone behind him.

Alex stood with a crooked smile, pointing a pepperbox pistol at him.

"Give me any reason," she said.

Jerry finally spoke. "Did you tell them?"

He let the question hang, then kept going.

"Did you tell them you killed an innocent man?" Jerry asked.

"That your name is really Reginald? That you're just a rich trust-fund baby using a motorcycle gang like a toy?" Greg asked.

Murmurs rippled through the group. Two shapes emerged from the gloom.

Sam stepped into the light, a Glock .40 raised and steady, pointed at one of the bikers.

"Yes," she said. "It's all true."

Alex leaned close and whispered to the man she was pointing the gun at, "She's telling the truth."

The biker swallowed hard.

Then engines roared again, this time not in defiance, but retreat.

One by one, bikes turned and rode off over the ridge. Some men tore their cuts loose and threw them aside as they went.

Ringo stood alone now, the circle emptying around him.

Greg, Alex, Sam, and Lucia faded back into the darkness, leaving Jerry and Ringo facing each other, the myth stripped bare, the night suddenly very quiet.

Ringo sneered first, leaning back as if the world owed him comfort.

"Jerry, you walk like a man who's already been buried, just too dumb to lie down. All that talk about honor and friends, but you smell like fear wrapped in cheap leather."

Jerry didn't raise his voice. He smiled. "Funny, Ringo. You dress like a king and talk like a legend, but everyone knows you're just a small man hiding behind louder men and dirtier tricks. Your name rides farther than you ever will."

Ringo laughed, sharp and hollow. "At least my name rides. Yours drags behind you, tied to every bad choice you ever made. And your friend, wrong place, wrong weakness. That's how it goes."

Jerry stepped closer. "Don't lie to yourself, Johnny. He wasn't weak. He was clean. He trusted the wrong man."

Ringo's eyes narrowed. "You think that makes you righteous? Men overdose every day. I didn't put the needle in his arm."

"No," Jerry said quietly. "You just put the poison in his hand."

There was a gust of wind.

"You're like a poor marksman. You were aiming at Colt," Jerry went on. "You missed, and Mark took the hit. Innocent men die when cowards set traps and pretend they're not responsible."

Ringo spat on the ground. "Careful, Jerry. Mouths like yours get buried."

Jerry held his stare. "Maybe. But Mark's already in the ground because of you. And no amount of noise, money, or muscle is going to bury that."

Ringo smiled thinly. "You think people will remember him?"

Jerry didn't hesitate. "They'll remember he was trying to live. And they'll remember you were trying to profit.

"Latin doesn't make you timeless, Johnny. It just gives hypocrites something to repeat. You've described yourself as the hero of a tragedy you don't understand. Read *The Tempest.* Prospero at least knew when to stop pretending."

For a moment, Ringo only stared at him.

Then the smile left his face.

The pistol came out smooth and practiced, not rushed, like he'd already decided how this ended.

Jerry didn't flinch. His hand dropped, and his own gun cleared just as clean.

Neither spoke.

Jerry's eyes narrowed.

Every fiber of his being wanted to pull the trigger. The urge rose fast and familiar, the same way the monster of addiction used to whisper *just one more.* He knew if he fired, no one would blame him. Not after Mark. Not after everything.

That was when he understood.

The hunger for justice had become its own addiction.

Jerry exhaled. Then he threw the pistol away. It hit the dirt and skidded away.

Ringo stared, stunned.

"No," Jerry said quietly. "I let myself destroy myself once. Mark is dead. But I won't let you take another life. You may kill me, but I'll die sober. That's something no one, not even you, can take from me."

He turned his back.

"Face me, you coward!" Ringo shouted.

Jerry kept walking.

"Face me, you junkie!" Ringo screamed.

Jerry mounted his bike and kicked it to life. He turned it slowly, deliberately.

Ringo raised his pistol. "No one walks away from me."

Jerry gunned the engine. Dirt and dust blasted into Ringo's face. He raised an arm to shield his eyes, then watched Jerry's taillight go over the rise. The rumble of a truck started somewhere.

Then, as the motorcycle engine faded, it seemed to grow louder.

A motorcycle crested the ridge, roaring down like a wave of steel and fire.

Johnny smiled. He recognized the engine's sound. It stopped just far enough that he could make out the silhouette of a chopper.

They split around Jerry as he rode uphill, then closed in behind him.

The rider dismounted and walked forward into the ring of light caused by Johnny's bike.

"I know what you did," Colt replied. "You tried to set me up. I brought you something."

He pulled out the Confederate bills.

"You really thought I wouldn't notice? I only gave the originals to one man. The masters were missing one. You didn't think that through." Colt's eyes hardened. "Jerry brought me the burned end of the missing original."

Ringo smiled weakly. "What are you going to do about it?"

Colt drew his pistol and fired.

Ringo hit the ground dead.

Colt stepped closer and fired once more into the body, then lowered his gun.

"Johnny, you always loved your Latin. *Actus non verba.* Action, not words."

ABOUT THE AUTHOR

JW Orchard is the creator of the PROACTIVE Agents series. They are fast-paced espionage thrillers set in real-world locations and featuring modern technological conflict. JW Orchard is a military veteran, world traveler, and international author. His stories explore what happens when power moves faster than law, and when doing the right thing comes at a cost. He personally researches the settings of his novels, traveling across the country to capture the landscapes, culture, and atmosphere that shape each mission. JW Orchard researches the real-world locations featured in his novels, traveling to places like Tombstone, Deadwood, Yellowstone, and New Orleans to bring authenticity to every mission. His work blends modern intelligence operations with moral tension and cinematic action.

They can be found at JWOrchardBooks.com.

ALSO, BY

JW ORCHARD

PROACTIVE Agents series
Ghost Hunters
Aces & Eights
Veil of Chains
Dance of Shadows
Plato O Plomo

Oceans of Fire series
Oceans of Fire
Poseidon's Hammer

Out of Purgatory series
Out of Purgatory
Divine Liturgy
Requiem for Elysium

www.ingramcontent.com/pod-product-compliance
Lightning Source LLC
LaVergne TN
LVHW010657110826
845149LV00014B/3140
9781970802139